JUSTICE AND ATONEMENT

Phoenix Lovegrove

COPYRIGHT

This work is a work of fiction. Names, characters, businesses, organisations, places, events, and incidents are either the products of the author's imagination or used in a fictitious manner. Any resemblance to actual persons, living or dead, or actual events is purely coincidental.

No part of this publication may be reproduced, distributed, or transmitted in any form or by any means, including photocopying, recording, or other electronic or mechanical methods, without the prior written permission of the Author or the Publisher, except in the case of brief quotations embodied in critical reviews and certain other non-commercial uses permitted by copyright law.

For permission requests, email the Author / Publisher on the address below:

Email: info@neuvare.com

Author page: www.phoenixlovegrove.neuvare.com

Publisher Website: www.neuvare.com

Book Cover by Neuvare

First edition: 2024

DISCLAIMER

This is a work of fiction. Names, characters, businesses, places, events, and incidents are either the products of the author's imagination or used in a fictitious manner. Any resemblance to actual persons, living or dead, or actual events is purely coincidental.

The publisher and author make no representations or warranties with respect to the accuracy or completeness of the contents of this book and specifically disclaim any implied warranties of merchantability or fitness for a particular purpose. Neither the publisher nor the author shall be liable for any loss of profit or any other commercial damages, including but not limited too special, incidental, consequential, or other damages.

The opinions and views expressed in this book are solely those of the fictional characters and do not necessarily reflect the views or opinions of the author or publisher.

This book contains mature content, including violence, strong language, and is intended for adult readers only.

SHARE YOUR EXPERIENCE

Dear Esteemed Reader,

I am thrilled to extend my deepest gratitude to you for selecting my book from the vast array of options available. Your decision to embark on this literary journey fills my heart with profound appreciation and excitement.

As you immerse yourself in the pages of this book, I hope you find yourself transported into the world I've crafted, drawn to the characters, and engaged by the unfolding narrative. Your experience as a reader is invaluable, and I would be honoured if you could spare a moment to share your thoughts.

Reviews serve as the lifeblood of any writer's career. They offer not only invaluable feedback but also guide other readers in discovering this book amidst the multitude of options available. Whether you choose to share a brief sentiment or provide a detailed analysis, your honest opinion holds immeasurable significance.

If the book resonates with you, I kindly invite you to consider leaving a review on the platform where you acquired or encountered this book. Your support in spreading the word would be immensely appreciated.

Conversely, if the book did not meet your expectations, I welcome your constructive criticism. Such feedback enables me to evolve and improve as a writer, ensuring that future works better align with the desires of my readers.

Once again, I extend my sincerest gratitude for your time, attention, and willingness to embark on this literary voyage with me. Your support fuels my passion for storytelling, and I am deeply grateful for each reader who joins me on this adventure.

Warm regards,

Phoenix Lovegrove

Author of Justice and Atonement

TABLE OF CONTENTS

CHAPTER ONE

Enigma

THE CITY OF Seattle stretched before Dr. Jessica McClain's eyes, its skyline piercing the brooding clouds above, a kaleidoscope of steel and glass. From the vantage point of her office window, the bustling metropolis seemed to pulse with a life of its own, oblivious to the complexities that lay within the walls of Emerald Harbour Medical Centre.

Jessica's gaze drifted from the city-scape to the stack of medical files on her desk, each one a reminder of the challenges she faced on a daily basis. As a neurologist, at one of the city's most prestigious hospitals, she had seen her fair share of puzzling cases. But one of them before her, seemed to defy conventional wisdom.

The patient's name was Ethan Parker, a vibrant twelve-year-old boy whose life had taken an inexplicable turn. Just weeks ago, Ethan had been a typical preteen, excelling in school and enjoying the carefree moments of childhood. But now, he was trapped in a world of confusion and disorientation, his once-brilliant mind, a shadow of its former self.

Jessica flipped through the pages of Ethan's file; her brow furrowed in concentration. The symptoms were perplexing — sudden memory lapses, episodes of disorientation, and an overall cognitive decline that defied explanation. Conventional tests had yielded no answers, leaving both Ethan's parents and the medical team grasping at straws.

A soft knock at the door broke Jessica's reverie, and she looked up to find her colleague and mentor, Dr. Michael Bennett, standing in the doorway. Lines of experience, etched his face, reflecting the weight of the countless lives he had touched throughout his illustrious career as a neurosurgeon.

"Jess, do you have a moment?" Michael's voice carried a hint of concern, a tone Jessica had grown accustomed to over the years.

"Of course Michael," she replied, gesturing for him to enter. "I was just going over Ethan Parker's file again."

Michael's expression darkened as he settled into the chair across from her desk. "I've been reviewing the case as well. It's unlike anything I've encountered before."

Jessica nodded, her fingers drumming lightly against the polished wood surface. "That's what worries me. We've ruled out the obvious culprits — tumours, infections, trauma — but there's something else at play here, something we're missing."

Michael leaned forward, his elbows resting on his knees. "Have you considered the possibility of a genetic component? Some of the symptoms could point to a rare neurological disorder."

"I've thought about that," Jessica admitted, "but

Ethan's family history doesn't suggest any genetic predisposition. Besides, the onset and progression of his condition don't align with what we know about most inherited disorders."

A heavy silence settled between them, punctuated only by the muffled sounds of activity from the hallway beyond Jessica's office. It was a silence born of frustration, a shared acknowledgement of the mysteries that still lurked within the human brain, despite their collective knowledge and experience.

"We can't give up," Michael said finally, his voice tinged with determination. "Ethan deserves answers, and we owe it to him and his family to leave no stone unturned."

Jessica met his gaze, her resolve hardening. "You're right. We'll dig deeper, explore every avenue, and consult with specialists if necessary. Ethan's case may be an enigma, but we won't stop until we find the solution."

As she uttered those words, Jessica felt a familiar fire ignite within her — the same fire that had drawn her to the field of neurology in the first place. It was a passion for unravelling the mysteries of the mind, for pushing the boundaries of understanding, and for offering hope where others saw only darkness.

Little did she know that Ethan's case would be the catalyst for a journey that would test her resolve and challenge her beliefs in ways she could never have imagined.

The following days were a whirlwind of activity as Jessica and Michael assembled a team of specialists to tackle Ethan's case. They pored over test results, consulted with geneticists and neuropsychologists, and explored every potential avenue, no matter how unconventional.

Despite their efforts, the answers they sought remained elusive, frustratingly out of reach. It was as if Ethan's condition existed in a realm beyond their current understanding, a puzzle with missing pieces that defied logic.

As the days stretched into weeks, Jessica found herself increasingly consumed by the case, spending long hours hunched over her desk, sifting through research papers and medical journals. She would often arrive at the hospital before dawn, fuelled by an unwavering determination to unlock the secrets that lay dormant within Ethan's brain.

On one such morning, Jessica sat alone in her office, the soft glow of her desk lamp casting an ethereal halo around her. The air was heavy with the scent of stale coffee, a testament to the countless hours she had spent poring over the enigmatic case.

A gentle rap at the door broke the silence, and Jessica looked up to find Dr. David Reynolds hovering in the doorway. A renowned neuropsychiatrist, David had been brought in to consult on Ethan's case, his expertise in cognitive and behavioural disorders proving invaluable.

"You're here early," David remarked, his voice laced with a hint of concern. "Have you been here all night?"

Jessica offered him a weary smile, brushing a stray lock of hair from her face. "I couldn't sleep. We are missing something David, and it's driving me crazy."

David stepped into the office, his eyes scanning the sea of papers and files that engulfed Jessica's desk. "We've explored every conventional avenue Jess. Maybe it's time we start thinking outside the box."

Jessica leaned back in her chair, her mind racing with possibilities. "What are you suggesting?"

Settling into the chair opposite her, David proposed. "Have you considered the role of environmental factors? An exposure to toxins, pollutants, or even electromagnetic fields could potentially trigger neurological disorders that defy our current understanding."

Jessica's brow furrowed as she considered his words. "It's a long shot, but at this point, we can't afford to ignore any potential lead."

David nodded, his expression grave. "There's something else we need to discuss — something that's been weighing on my mind."

Jessica sat up straight, sensing the gravity in his tone. "What is it?"

"Have you noticed any unusual behaviour from the pharmaceutical representatives who've been circling the hospital lately?" David asked, his voice lowered to a conspiratorial whisper.

Jessica's eyes narrowed. "You mean the ones pushing that new drug, Neuroloxyn? They've been relentless, but that's par for the course with big Pharma."

"That's just it," David pressed on, leaning forward. "From what I've heard, Neuroloxyn hasn't been thoroughly tested, and there are concerns about potential side effects — side effects that could mirror some of Ethan's symptoms."

A heavy silence hung between them as Jessica processed the implications of David's words. Could it be possible that Ethan's condition was somehow linked to the very drugs meant to treat neurological disorders?

"Are you suggesting that Ethan's been exposed to Neuroloxyn?" Jessica asked, her voice laced with disbelief.

David shrugged; his expression grim. "I don't know for sure, but it's a possibility we can't ignore. These pharmaceutical companies will stop at nothing to push their products, even if it means cutting corners on safety protocols."

Jessica felt a familiar sense of outrage bubbling within her. She had dedicated her life to healing, to alleviating suffering, and the notion that corporate greed could be compromising patient care was abhorrent to her.

"If what you're suggesting is true," she said, her voice trembling with barely contained fury, "then we're dealing with something far more insidious than a medical mystery."

David nodded solemnly. "Precisely, we need to tread carefully. These companies have deep pockets and powerful allies. If they catch wind of our suspicions, they'll do everything in their power to shut us down."

As the weight of David's words settled upon her, Jessica felt a renewed sense of determination coursing through her veins. She had sworn an oath to protect her patients, and she would not allow anyone — or anything — to stand in the way of that sacred duty.

"Then we keep digging," she declared, her jaw set in a firm line. "Whatever it takes, we'll get to the bottom of this. Ethan's life hangs in the balance, and I won't rest until we find the answers he deserves."

Jessica's quest took on a new urgency, fuelled by the suspicion that forces beyond her control were at play. She delved deeper into the world of pharmaceutical companies and their intricate web of influence, uncovering disturbing truths that threatened to shake the very foundations of her profession.

As the investigation progressed, Jessica found herself forming an unlikely alliance with David, their shared scepticism towards the pharmaceutical industry forging an unbreakable bond. Together, they navigated a treacherous landscape of corporate greed and medical ethics, determined to expose the truth, no matter the cost.

Unbeknownst to them, their actions had not gone unnoticed. Lurking in the shadows, were those pharmaceutical reps who had been circling the hospital, watching their every move. Driven by an unquenchable thirst for money and the eager anticipation of securing that next lucrative deal, their motives remained inexorable.

As the days ticked by, the stakes grew higher, and the lines between right and wrong became increasingly blurred. Jessica found herself questioning everything she thought she knew, her once-unwavering faith in the medical establishment slowly eroding.

Yet, through it all, Ethan's plight remained her guiding light. The young boy's haunting eyes, once filled with life and promise, now dulled by the ravages of his condition, served as a constant reminder of the gravity of her mission.

With each passing day, Jessica inched closer to the

truth, her determination fuelled by a burning desire for justice. She knew that the road ahead would be fraught with obstacles, but she was prepared to face them head-on, no matter the personal cost.

In the shadows of the mind, a battle was raging — a battle for the very soul of medicine itself. Jessica was determined to be the one who emerged victorious, a beacon of hope in a world where the lines between healing and harm had become dangerously blurred.

CHAPTER TWO

Descent into Darkness

THE REVELATIONS ABOUT Neuroloxyn and the potential involvement of pharmaceutical companies in Ethan's condition weighed heavily on Jessica's mind. As she delved deeper into the investigation, she stumbled upon a treacherous landscape of corporate greed and ethical compromises.

Her once-unwavering faith in the medical establishment was slowly eroding, replaced by a growing sense of disillusionment. She had dedicated her life to the pursuit of healing, and the thought that corporations could be putting profits before patient safety was a bitter pill to swallow.

In the weeks that followed, Jessica and David worked tirelessly, poring over research papers and medical journals, searching for any clue that could shed light on Ethan's condition and its potential connection to Neuroloxyn.

Their investigation led them down a twisted path, revealing disturbing findings about the lengths pharmaceutical companies were willing to go to ensure their products' success. They uncovered suspicions of clinical trials being manipulated, adverse side effects being downplayed, and regulatory agencies turning a blind eye to questionable practices.

As the pieces of the puzzle began to fall into place, Jessica found herself consumed by a sense of righteous anger.

Amid her growing disillusionment, Jessica found comfort in her work with Ethan. As she watched him slip further into the shadows of his mind, her determination to find answers only grew stronger.

David too, remained steadfast in his commitment to the cause, his unwavering support providing a much-needed source of strength for Jessica. Their unbreakable alliance, united them in a quest for truth and justice.

However, their actions did not go unnoticed. Whispers began to circulate within the hallowed halls of Emerald Harbour Medical Centre, murmurs of discontent from those who saw their investigation as a threat to the status quo.

It was during one of their clandestine meetings that Jessica and David first became aware of the forces arrayed against them. They had gathered in a secluded corner of the hospital cafeteria; their hushed voices barely audible over the din of clinking cutlery and idle chatter.

"We need to be careful," David warned, his eyes darting around the room as if searching for unseen threats. "Word is getting out about our investigation, and some people are getting nervous."

Jessica's brow furrowed, her fingers tightening around the steaming mug of coffee she clutched. "Who exactly is getting nervous?"

David leaned in closer, his voice dropping to a

conspiratorial whisper. "The pharmaceutical reps, for starters. They've been making inquiries, asking questions about our involvement in Ethan's case."

A chill ran down Jessica's spine as the implications of David's words sank in. They had stumbled upon something far bigger than they had initially anticipated, something that threatened to shake the very foundations of the medical establishment.

"Are you suggesting they're trying to intimidate us?" she asked, her voice laced with disbelief.

David nodded grimly. "It wouldn't be the first time. These companies have deep pockets and powerful allies. They'll do whatever it takes to protect their interests."

Jessica felt a surge of defiance rise within her; a fiery determination that had been forged in the crucible of her profession. She had taken an oath and dedicated her life to healing, to alleviating suffering, and she would not be cowed by the machinations of those who sought to put profits before patients.

"Let them try," she declared, her eyes blazing with resolve. "We're not backing down, not when so much is at stake."

David nodded, a ghost of a smile playing across his lips. "I knew you'd say that. You're a force to be reckoned with Jess."

Jessica and David's investigation took on a new

urgency, fuelled by the knowledge that they were treading on dangerous ground. They redoubled their efforts, working tirelessly to uncover the truth, no matter the cost.

As the weeks rolled into months, the walls seemed too close in around them. Whispers in the hallways grew louder, and sidelong glances from colleagues became more frequent. It was as if a dark cloud had descended upon Emerald Harbour Medical Centre, casting a pall over their once-noble pursuit of healing.

Through it all, Jessica remained steadfast, her resolve unwavering as she drew strength from Ethan's plight, from the haunting image of the once-vibrant boy trapped deep in the shadows of his mind.

In the darkest moments, when the weight of their mission threatened to overwhelm her, Jessica would steal away to Ethan's bedside. She would sit beside him, observing the tranquil rhythm of his breathing, a stark reminder of why she had chosen this path.

It was during one of these vigils that a breakthrough occurred, a glimmer of hope amidst the gathering darkness. Jessica had been poring over Ethan's medical records, searching for any detail, no matter how minute, that could shed light on his condition.

It was then that she noticed a peculiar notation, a

seemingly innocuous detail that they had overlooked in their previous examinations. Ethan's doctor had prescribed him Neuroadoxyn, a medication for a minor ailment a few weeks before his symptoms started. Zooth Pharmaceuticals, a Fortune 500 pharmaceutical empire behind Neuroloxyn, also developed and marketed Neuroadoxyn.

Jessica's heart raced as she pieced together the implications. Could it be possible that Ethan's condition was a result of an adverse reaction to the medication, one that had gone unnoticed or intentionally downplayed by the company in their rush to bring their product to market?

With trembling hands, she reached for her phone, her fingers fumbling as she dialled David's number. When he answered, his voice tinged with concern, she could barely contain her excitement.

"David, I think I found something," she breathed, her words tumbling out in a rush. "It's a connection, a link between Ethan's case and one of the pharmaceutical companies we've been investigating."

There was a pause on the other end of the line, and Jessica could almost hear the cogwheels turning in David's head.

"Tell me everything," he said finally, his tone grave.

As Jessica laid out her findings, she could sense the

weight of the moment bearing down upon them. They had uncovered a thread, a tenuous thread that could unravel the entire tapestry of deceit and corruption that had ensnared them.

Their investigation took on a newfound sense of urgency. They pored over medical records, cross-referenced data, and consulted with experts from around the world, determined to leave no stone unturned.

As the pieces of the puzzle began to fall into place, a chilling picture emerged — one of corporate greed and disregard for human life, all in the pursuit of profit.

It became increasingly clear that Ethan's condition was merely the tip of the iceberg, a symptom of a far more insidious disease that had taken root within the medical establishment.

Yet, even as they inched closer to the truth, the shadows seemed to grow longer, the forces arrayed against them more formidable. Whispers in the hallways gave way to veiled threats, and Jessica found herself the target of thinly veiled intimidation tactics.

With unwavering determination, she pressed on, fuelled by a burning desire for justice. She knew that the road ahead would be fraught with obstacles, but she was prepared to face them head-on, no matter the personal cost.

For in the shadows of her mind, a battle was raging

— a battle for the very soul of medicine itself. Dr Jessica McClain was determined to forge on and emerge victorious, a beacon of hope in a world where the lines between healing and harm had become dangerously blurred.

As the sun set over Seattle, casting long shadows across the city, Jessica stood at her office window, her gaze fixed on the distant horizon. The road ahead was shrouded in uncertainty, but she would not rest until the truth was laid bare.

With a steely resolve, she turned away from the window, her mind already focused on the challenges that lay ahead. The descent into darkness had begun, and she was prepared to face it head-on, armed with the knowledge that her cause was just and that the lives of countless patients hung in the balance.

In the end, it was not just about Ethan or any single case — it was about restoring integrity to a system that had been corrupted and reclaiming the sacred bond between healers and those they had sworn to protect.

As Jessica stepped out into the dimly lit hallway, she felt a newfound sense of purpose burn within her. The battle lines had been drawn, and she was ready to wage war against the forces that threatened to extinguish the very essence of what it meant to be a doctor.

CHAPTER THREE

Wolves in Sheep's Clothing

DEEP WITHIN THE sleek, high-rise headquarters of Zooth Pharmaceuticals, a storm was brewing. The opulent boardroom, with its polished mahogany table and floor-to-ceiling windows overlooking the Miami skyline, had been transformed into a battleground, where the stakes were measured not in territorial gains but in profits and reputations.

At the head of the table sat 55 year old Gavin Caldwell, the company's CEO – a man whose sharp features and piercing gaze belied a ruthless ambition that had propelled him to the pinnacle of the pharmaceutical industry. Flanked on either side by a cadre of executives and legal advisors, was:

- 60 year old Dante Underhill, the company's CFO,

- 49 year old Rajesh Patel, Chief Medical Officer,

- 46 year old Griffin Kesser, VP Regulatory Affairs,

- 38 year old Nova Hollingsworth, VP Marketing,

- 53 year old Atlas Jenner, VP Manufacturing,

- 62 year old Wallace Tanaka, VP East Asia Operations,

- 48 year old Haruki Aso, VP West Asia

Operations – Tanaka's counterpart for Zooth's Indian operations,

- 51 year old Heinrich Gerken, VP European Operations

- 43 year old Lyra Velazquez, Chief Legal Officer

Gavin Caldwell presided over the proceedings with an iron fist, his every word carrying the weight of authority.

The atmosphere was tense, charged with an undercurrent of barely contained fury. The news of Dr McClain and Dr Reynolds' investigation had sent shockwaves through the corridors of power, prompting an emergency board meeting to address the looming threat.

"Gentlemen, ladies," Caldwell began, his voice cutting through the silence like a well-honed blade. "We have a situation on our hands, one that threatens to undermine everything we've worked so hard to achieve."

A murmur of discontent rippled through the room, as the assembled executives exchanged furtive glances. They knew all too well the implications of Caldwell's words — an investigation into Zooth Pharmaceuticals could spell disaster for the company, jeopardising the very products they had poured billions into developing.

"Our pharmaceutical representatives have brought

to our attention a troubling development," Caldwell continued, his steely gaze sweeping across the room. "It seems that two doctors at Emerald Harbour Medical Centre, a Dr Jessica McClain and a Dr David Reynolds, have taken it upon themselves to launch an unauthorised investigation into our latest breakthrough drug, Neuroloxyn."

At the mention of the drug's name, a palpable tension settled over the room. Neuroloxyn was the crown jewel of Zooth Pharmaceuticals arsenal, a cutting-edge treatment for neurological disorders that promised to revolutionise the field of medicine — and generate billions in revenue for the company.

"These doctors have raised concerns about potential side effects and have even suggested that Neuroloxyn may be linked to a recent case involving a young patient," Caldwell said, his voice laced with contempt. "This is not only reckless but potentially damaging to our company's reputation and bottom line."

A wave of murmurs and hushed conversations spread through the room, as the executives grappled with the seriousness of the situation. Some displayed expressions of disbelief, while others seemed resigned to the inevitability of challenges in the competitive world of pharmaceuticals.

"This cannot go unchallenged," Caldwell

exclaimed, his fist striking the polished tabletop with a resounding thud. "We've invested too much, sacrificed too greatly, to allow a pair of misguided doctors to disrupt our plans."

A tense silence descended upon the room as Caldwell's words hung in the air. The executives knew his resolve well — he was both revered and feared for his unwavering dedication to the company's interests.

"Our legal team is already preparing a robust defence," Caldwell declared, his tone revealing a steely determination. "We'll refute all allegations and launch a counter-offensive to discredit these doctors and their unfounded claims."

A ripple of murmurs passed through the room as the executives pondered over Caldwell's strategy. They were aware that such tactics were commonplace in the world of big Pharma, where reputations could be made or shattered in an instant.

"But that's not all," Caldwell continued, his gaze hardening. "We need to take a more proactive stance, one that sends a clear message to anyone daring to oppose us."

A hush fell over the room as the executives leaned in, intrigued by Caldwell's next move.

"Our representatives are already applying pressure, subtly reminding these doctors of the consequences," Caldwell explained, his voice low and menacing. "But we must be prepared to take more drastic measures if needed."

A collective gasp echoed through the room as Caldwell's words sank in. They all understood the unspoken truth — in the world of big Pharma, profits often outweighed ethics, and dissenters were swiftly dealt with.

"We have the means and connections to make life difficult for these doctors," Caldwell asserted, his eyes flashing with determination. "If they persist, we'll use our influence without hesitation."

A heavy silence lingered, broken only by the rustle of papers. The executives knew they were entering dangerous territory but yielding to the demands of a few renegade doctors was out of the question.

"Understand this," Caldwell declared firmly. "We're not just sellers of medication; we're pioneers of progress, bringing hope to millions. Surrendering now would betray our shareholders and the very essence of our industry."

Nods and murmurs of agreement filled the room as the executives rallied behind Caldwell's vision. They weren't mere corporate figures; they were the vanguards of progress, fighting against suffering with the tools of science and innovation.

"We'll endure this storm, as we've done before," Caldwell proclaimed, his voice filled with conviction. "And when it's over, we'll emerge stronger and more committed than ever to our cause."

With those words, the executives rose, faces set with determination, ready to unleash their corporate power against any threat to their dominance.

As they filed out of the boardroom, their footsteps echoing against the polished marble floors, they were no longer mere businessmen and women — they were soldiers in a war for hearts and minds, armed with weapons of influence and intimidation.

In the days and weeks that followed, the shadows began to lengthen around Jessica and David, as the full weight of Zooth Pharmaceuticals' retaliatory campaign began to take shape.

Whispers and innuendo flooded the hallways of Emerald Harbour Medical Centre, casting doubt on the integrity of their investigation and their motives. Suddenly, their once-respected colleagues seemed distant, their gazes averting as the two doctors passed by.

Subtle threats began to emerge, veiled in the guise of friendly warnings or innocuous inquiries. Anonymous notes would appear on their desks, their contents hinting at the dire consequences that awaited those who dared to challenge the status quo.

Yet, despite the mounting pressure, Jessica and David remained resolute, their determination fuelled by a burning sense of righteous indignation.

They had sworn an oath to protect their patients, and they would not be cowed by the machinations of those who valued profits over human lives.

As they dug deeper into the web of deceit surrounding Neuroloxyn, they encountered obstacle after obstacle, each one more daunting than the last. Research data was mysteriously lost, or corrupted, key witnesses disappeared or recanted their testimonies, and doors that had once been open were now firmly closed.

But for every setback, they found new allies — doctors, researchers, and whistle-blowers who had seen first-hand the insidious tentacles of corporate greed infiltrating the hallowed halls of medicine. These unlikely allies provided crucial information, bolstering Jessica and David's case and lending credence to their suspicions.

As the battle raged on, the lines between ally and adversary became increasingly blurred. Friendships were tested, loyalties were questioned, and the very foundations of trust upon which the medical community was built began to crumble.

In the midst of this maelstrom, Jessica and David found solace in each other's unwavering support. Their bond, forged in the fires of their shared crusade, grew stronger with each passing day, a bulwark against the forces arrayed against them.

Yet, even as their resolve hardened, the shadows around them grew longer, the threats more tangible. Incidents that had once been dismissed as mere coincidence took on a more sinister cast, as the spectre of corporate retaliation loomed ever larger.

***

It was a rain-swept night that would forever be seared into Jessica's memory, a night when the stakes of her crusade against Zooth Pharmaceuticals became brutally, inescapably real. As she made her way across the deserted hospital parking lot, the cold rain pelting her face, Jessica's mind raced with the damning evidence she had uncovered about Neuroloxyn's deadly side effects.

So consumed was she by her thoughts that she didn't notice the dark figure materialising from the shadows until he was right in front of her. Jessica gasped, her heart seizing as she came face-to-face with a man whose features were obscured by the inky blackness. Before she could react, he spoke in a chilling, distorted growl.

"You're playing a dangerous game, Doctor. It's time to back off before you get yourself hurt."

A chill ran down Jessica's spine, but she refused to show fear in front of this menacing stranger. Squaring her shoulders, she met his concealed gaze with an unwavering stare. "Is that a threat?"

The figure let out a low, grating chuckle that seemed to reverberate in the rain-soaked air around them. "Consider it a friendly warning. You and your partner have poked the bear one too many times. Back off or face the consequences."

Jessica felt her heart pounding, the adrenaline firing through her veins as the weight of the man's words washed over her. But she wasn't cowed — if anything, she felt a renewed sense of resolve burning within her.

With a final ominous look, the shadowy figure melted back into the night, leaving Jessica alone in the rain. She stood there for a long moment, rain plastering her hair to her skin, trying to process what had just happened. Whoever that man was, whatever depths of depravity he represented, Jessica knew one thing — she had crossed a line tonight from which there was no going back.

The drive home passed by in a blur, her white-knuckled hands gripping the steering wheel as the ghostly words of the parking lot stranger echoed in her mind. By the time she arrived at her apartment, Jessica had come to a decision. There would be no turning back, no cutting her losses and fading into the night to preserve her own safety. Not after tonight, not after seeing the face of the malign forces arrayed against her with her own eyes.

No, from this night forward, Jessica vowed to herself that she would pursue this case until its ultimate conclusion, until justice was served no matter how high the casualties or personal cost. Zooth Pharmaceuticals and their mercenary enforcers could threaten, intimidate, and try to instil fear — but they would not shake her resolve. Not now, not ever.

As she climbed into bed, the rain still lashing at the windows, Jessica felt an eerie sense of calm settle over her. She knew the road ahead would be fraught with peril, possibly even costing her everything she cherished most. But some causes were worth sacrificing for. Some evils demanded confronting, no matter what lines had to be crossed.

This was her Rubicon, and there was no going back. Zooth's crimes against humanity would be exposed, by any means necessary. Jessica closed her eyes, letting the patter of the rain lull her into a restless sleep, her last thoughts of the long, dark journey that lay ahead.

CHAPTER FOUR

Open concern

THE NEWS OF Jessica's harrowing encounter in the parking lot spread like wildfire through the corridors of Emerald Harbour Medical Centre. Perhaps she was onto something – maybe there was truth to the rumours she and David had been quietly investigating. What had begun as muffled speculation and furtive exchanges rapidly escalated into vocal apprehension and indignation among the staff. The once-hushed whispers and furtive glances had given way to overt expressions of open concern and outrage?

Nurses huddled in small groups, brows furrowed in discussion. Doctors paused in the corridors, shaking their heads grimly. Even the usually unflappable administrators were heard voicing their concern, their voices carrying an uncharacteristic edge of alarm.

Something was clearly amiss. Could the investigation they had been quietly conducting finally shed light on the inexplicable occurrences that had long plagued the facility? The once-docile doctors and nurses were no longer content to confine their concerns to hushed discussions behind closed doors. The peaceful veneer that had cloaked Emerald Harbour Medical Centre had been shattered, replaced by a pervasive sense of unease and a determination to uncover the truth.

Colleagues who had once distanced themselves from Jessica and David's investigation now rallied around them, their eyes wide with disbelief at the lengths Zooth Pharmaceuticals was willing to go to protect their interests.

As Jessica's harrowing story began to filter out of the confines of Emerald Harbour Medical Centre, a palpable shift occurred within the hospital ranks. The once-impenetrable wall of silence and complicity began to crack, as more and more members of the medical community found their voices and joined the chorus of dissent.

Amid this growing maelstrom, Jessica and David remained hardened by the knowledge that they were no longer fighting alone. They now had allies and had become symbols of resistance, a beacon of hope for those who had long feared the repercussions of speaking out against the pharmaceutical industry's excesses.

Yet, even as their ranks swelled, the situation took on an increasingly dire tone. For Ethan Parker, the young patient whose plight had sparked this crusade, time was running out.

Despite their best efforts, his condition continued to deteriorate, his once-vibrant mind slipping further into the shadows with each passing day. The medical team watched helplessly as Ethan's cognitive functions declined, his once-brilliant smile fading into a vacant stare that chilled the heart.

As Jessica sat by Ethan's bedside, her hand enveloping his small, frail fingers, she couldn't help but feel a profound sense of urgency. This was no longer just a battle for truth and justice; it was a race against the clock, a desperate bid to unravel the mysteries that threatened to claim an innocent life.

It was during one of these vigils that Jessica received a call from David that would change the course of their investigation forever.

"Jess, you need to come to my office, immediately," his voice tinged with a mixture of excitement and trepidation, crackled through the phone's speaker.

Jessica's brow furrowed at the urgency in her colleague's tone. "What's going on David?"

There was a pause, a pregnant silence that seemed to stretch for an eternity. "It's happening again," he said finally. "And this time, it's not just Ethan."

A chill ran down Jessica's spine as the implications of David's words sank in. Could it be that their worst fears were being realised? That Ethan's condition was not an isolated incident, but rather the harbinger of a much larger crisis?

Without a moment's hesitation, Jessica rose from Ethan's bedside, her fingers gently disentangling themselves from the boy's grasp. She knew, at that moment, that their fight had taken on a new dimension — one that transcended the boundaries of Emerald Harbour Medical Centre and threatened to engulf the entire medical community.

As she hurried through the bustling corridors, her mind raced with possibilities, each more dire than the last. Had Zooth Pharmaceuticals' reckless pursuit of profits unleashed a medical catastrophe of unprecedented proportions? And if so, how far did the tentacles of their deceit truly reach?

When she arrived at David's office, the gravity of the situation became painfully clear. Scattered across his desk were files, each one bearing the redacted name of a patient — patients from across the country, all exhibiting symptoms eerily similar to Ethan's.

"A single occurrence could be chalked up to chance, but when faced with a multitude of them, attributing them all to coincidence becomes increasingly implausible," David said, his voice laced with a mixture of outrage and disbelief. "These cases are too widespread, too consistent to be anything but a pattern."

Jessica's fingers trembled as she leafed through the files, her eyes scanning the pages with mounting horror. Each patient's story was a testament to the insidious reach of Zooth Pharmaceuticals' machinations, a stark reminder of the human cost of corporate greed.

As they delved deeper into the files, a chilling picture began to emerge — one that painted Neuroloxyn, not as a breakthrough treatment but as a ticking time bomb, a harbinger of devastating side effects that had been deliberately downplayed or outright concealed.

With each new case they uncovered, the weight of their responsibility grew heavier, like a crushing burden upon their shoulders. They were no longer merely fighting for one patient or one hospital; they had become warriors in a battle for the very soul of the medical profession.

Despite a crisis becoming evident, those opposing them increased their efforts to keep the secrecy intact. In an attempt to control public anger, whistleblowers were silenced, data was suppressed, and a deliberate misinformation campaign was initiated.

Jessica and David had inadvertently stumbled upon a Pandora's box, unwittingly thrusting themselves into a battlefield scattered across several fronts. On one side, they fought to unravel the web of deceit surrounding Neuroloxyn, piecing together the fragments of truth that had been scattered to the winds. On the other, they battled against a relentless onslaught of intimidation and threats, with their every move scrutinised by the ever-watchful eyes of Zooth Pharmaceuticals' enforcers.

The stress began to take its toll on Jessica, both physically and emotionally. She would often find herself staring into the mirror, her eyes haunted by the weight of the burden she carried. Dark circles etched themselves beneath her once-vibrant gaze, a testament to the countless nights spent poring over files.

David also bore the scars of their crusade, his once-jovial demeanour giving way to a grim determination that seemed to emanate from the very core of his being. Together, they forged ahead, undaunted by the obstacles that loomed before them, driven by a shared conviction that they were fighting for something larger than themselves.

As the calendar pages flipped and the months seamlessly transitioned from one to another, the trickle of redacted cases continued to flow in, revealing a stream of harrowing tales that threatened to overwhelm even the most stalwart of souls. News of their investigation crossed the boarders and soon cases began to flow in from abroad. With every fresh document, with every narrative of a new patient, it served as a poignant testament to the toll exacted by corporate avarice and institutional misconduct.

And then, the unthinkable happened — the first reports of fatalities from abroad began to surface.

What began as a whisper, a rumour passed along in hushed tones among the medical community. Soon began to spread, the whispers became shouts, and the shouts became a deafening roar that could no longer be ignored.

Patients whose conditions had once been treatable, and manageable, had succumbed to the devastating side effects of Neuroloxyn, their lives snuffed out like candles in the wind. The toll was staggering, a body count that grew with each passing day, a grim testament to the consequences of prioritising profits over human lives.

As the news reached Jessica and David, they found themselves plunged into the depths of despair. How many lives had been lost? How many families had been shattered by the callous disregard of a corporation driven by greed?

Fuelled by a righteous fury that burned like a beacon in the gathering darkness. They became voices for the voiceless, champions for those whose lives had been forever altered by the machinations of Zooth Pharmaceuticals.

Slowly, the floodgates began to open. One by one, redacted patient files, autopsy reports, emails, and memos began to flow in. Until a deluge of documents emerged. The weight of their staggering revelations threatened to drown Jessica and David beneath it. Each file held a shroud of secrecy, exposing the ugly truth about Neuroloxyn - a drug that had seemed innocuous enough on the surface, but now revealed itself as a silent killer on a scale Jessica and David could scarcely comprehend. The death toll mounting with every redacted document.

But it wasn't until leaked emails and internal memos began to trickle in from disgruntled employees of Zooth Pharmaceuticals, that the nightmarish reality began to take shape, — a reality where the staggering number of lives claimed by this unassuming pill dwarfed even the most pessimistic projections. Each incriminating document left a grisly trail of breadcrumbs leading to the doorstep of Zooth Pharmaceuticals. With each damning revelation, the staggering magnitude of Neuroloxyn's deadly side effects became more inescapable, more horrifically real.

Jessica and David were sitting on a powder keg of evidence, and the fuse was burning rapidly.

As storm clouds gathered on the horizon, Jessica and David knew that the battle had only just begun. The road ahead was shrouded in uncertainty, littered with obstacles and perils that threatened to derail their crusade at every turn.

But in the face of such adversity, they remained resolute, their determination forged in the fires of their shared outrage. They knew that they were fighting for something larger than themselves — a fight for the very soul of the medical profession, a fight to restore the sacred trust between healers and those they had sworn to protect.

And as they stood together, shoulder to shoulder, they made a silent vow — a vow to see this through to the bitter end. For Jessica and David, there was no turning back — only the relentless pursuit of truth, no matter how dark the path before them might become.

CHAPTER FIVE

The Gathering Storm

WITHIN THE TOWERING edifice of Zooth Pharmaceuticals' headquarters, a palpable sense of unease permeated the air. The once-invincible aura of corporate might had been shaken to its core, as the allegations surrounding Neuroloxyn threatened to unravel the very fabric of the company's existence.

In the executive suite, a war council had convened, comprising of the company's top brass and a legion of lawyers and PR specialists. The opulent boardroom, overlooking the Miami skyline, had been transformed into a command centre, where strategies were plotted and battle-lines were drawn.

Leading the charge was Gavin Caldwell. With an ice-cold gaze, the CEO sized up his quarry. His eyes sweeping across the assembled throng. With his jaw set in a tight line and white knuckles, he gripped the arms of his chair, a silent testament to the fury simmering beneath his polished facade.

"Gentlemen, ladies," Caldwell began. His voice sliced through the tense silence with razor-sharp precision. "We still find ourselves amid the crisis with Dr McClain and Dr Reynolds".

"They have taken their full-scale assault on Zooth Pharmaceuticals and Neuroloxyn to the next level; they have not only gone national, they have gone global," Caldwell continued. His eyes narrowed into icy slits. "Their allegations of adverse side effects and potential links to patient deaths have gained traction. We are now facing scrutiny from regulatory bodies and the public at large."

The room filled with a collective gasp, as the gravity of Caldwell's words sank in. Neuroloxyn was the crown jewel of Zooth Pharmaceuticals' portfolio. To have that golden goose threatened by the actions of two rogue doctors was unthinkable, a scenario that struck at the very heart of the company's financial and reputational standing.

"We have taken measures to discredit these doctors and their claims," Caldwell pressed on, his voice laced with a steely resolve. "Our legal team has mounted a robust defence, and our public relations specialists have launched a counter-offensive to sway public opinion in our favour."

A chorus of nods rippled through the room, as the executives acknowledged the efforts already underway. They had played this game before, wielding the twin weapons of legal might and media manipulation to reshape narratives and silence dissent.

But this time, something was different. This time, the tide of public sentiment seemed to be turning against them, fuelled by a growing sense of outrage at the mounting evidence of corporate malfeasance.

"However," Caldwell said, his voice dropping to a conspiratorial whisper, "it has become clear that more... direct measures are required."

A hush fell over the room, as the assembled

executives leaned in, their curiosity piqued by the implications of Caldwell's words.

"Our adversaries have proven to be more resilient than anticipated," the CEO continued, his steely gaze sweeping across the room. "They have amassed a formidable body of evidence, and their network of allies seems to be growing by the day".

A ripple of unease coursed through the room, as the executives contemplated the ramifications of Caldwell's words. They had dealt with whistleblowers and dissenters before, but never on this scale, never with such far-reaching consequences.

"We cannot allow this threat to fester any longer," Caldwell declared, his voice ringing with conviction. "The time has come to take more aggressive action".

The atmosphere was thick with silence, broken only by sporadic rustles of paper or the subtle clearing of throats. They all knew the unspoken truth — that in the cutthroat world of big Pharma, the pursuit of profits often took precedence over ethical considerations, and those who stood in the way were dealt with swiftly and without mercy.

"Our intelligence has uncovered a growing network of doctors and medical professionals who have thrown their support behind Dr McClain and Dr Reynolds," Caldwell said, his eyes narrowing. "They are sharing data, compiling evidence, and preparing to take their case to the FDA."

A collective murmur of dismay rippled through the room, as the executives grappled with the implications of such a move. A full-scale investigation by the FDA could spell disaster for Neuroloxyn, potentially leading to the drug's withdrawal from the market and a crippling financial blow to the company.

"This cannot be allowed to happen," Caldwell growled, his fist slamming down on the polished tabletop with a resounding thud. "We have invested too much, sacrificed too much, to let a band of misguided idealists derail our plans."

The air grew thick with tension, as the executives braced themselves for the CEO's next move. They knew that Caldwell was a man accustomed to getting his way, a man who would stop at nothing to protect the interests of Zooth Pharmaceuticals.

"Our legal team has already begun preparing injunctions and cease-and-desist orders," Caldwell announced, his voice laced with a steely determination. "We will use every tool at our disposal to shut down this rogue network and stem the flow of information."

A ripple of unease coursed through the room, as the executives contemplated the implications of such a heavy-handed approach. They had played hardball before, but never on such a grand scale, never with such far-reaching consequences.

"But that is not all," Caldwell continued, his gaze hardening. "We must send a clear message to those who would dare to challenge us — a message that will resonate throughout the medical community and beyond ".

A hush fell over the room, as the executives leaned in, their curiosity mingled with a hint of trepidation at the implications of Caldwell's words.

"Our investigators have identified key players in this network, individuals who have proven to be particularly... troublesome," the CEO said, his voice dropping to a menacing whisper. "It is time we dealt with them directly."

A collective shiver ran through the room, as the assembled executives exchanged furtive glances. "We have the resources and the connections to make life very difficult for these individuals," Caldwell continued, his eyes blazing with a fierce determination. "If they persist in their foolish crusade, we will not hesitate to leverage our full influence to intervene decisively."

The atmosphere was thick with silence, broken only by sporadic rustles of paper or the subtle clearing of throats. The executives knew that they were treading on dangerous ground, but they also knew that the alternative — capitulating to the demands of a rogue network of medical professionals — was simply unacceptable.

"Make no mistake, my friends," Caldwell said, his

voice ringing with conviction. "We are not mere peddlers of pills; we are the vanguard of progress, the bearers of hope for millions who suffer from the ravages of disease and affliction. To surrender now would be to betray not only our shareholders but the very foundations upon which our industry was built."

A chorus of nods and murmurs of assent greeted Caldwell's impassioned words, as the executives rallied around the banner of their collective cause. They didn't see themselves as mere corporate cogs; rather, they considered themselves soldiers in a battle against suffering, equipped with the tools of science and innovation.

"We will weather this storm, as we have weathered countless others before," Caldwell declared. His voice resonating with almost messianic fervour. "And when the dust settles, we will emerge stronger, more resilient, and more committed than ever, to our mission".

With a shuffle of chairs, the executives rose from their seats, their faces etched with grim determination, ready to unleash the full force of their corporate might against the perceived threats to their dominance.

***

In the days and weeks that followed, the shadows began to lengthen around the network of doctors and medical professionals who had dared to challenge the might of Zooth Pharmaceuticals.

Legal manoeuvres were set in motion, as Zooth Pharmaceuticals army of lawyers unleashed a barrage of injunctions and cease-and-desist orders, each one designed to silence dissent and stem the flow of information.

Yet, despite the mounting pressure, the network continued to grow and remained resolute, their determination fuelled by a burning sense of righteous indignation.

The unwavering leadership of Dr Jessica McClain and Dr David Reynolds served as a beacon of hope for those who had joined their cause. They redoubled their efforts, coordinating the collection and dissemination of data, and forging alliances with like-minded individuals across the globe. Yet, even as their resolve hardened, the shadows around them grew longer, and the threats more tangible.

CHAPTER SIX

A Vow Sworn in Blood

Waking up to the sterile surroundings of an all too familiar emergency ward, David sat up and winced as he carefully peeled off the bloodstained bandages, revealing a jagged line of black stitches tracing down the side of his face and neck. An E.R. doctor approached. "You are a lucky man," he said. "A little deeper and that gash would have severed your carotid artery."

He gingerly touched the raised welt of purple and yellow bruising surrounding the fresh sutures, hissing in pain at even the slightest pressure. The memories of last night's vicious attack came flooding back in lurid flashes.

He had been driving home from Emerald Harbour Medical Centre, at around 11 pm after staying late to dig through more case files on Zooth Pharmaceuticals.

As he drove down the empty suburban street a few miles from his home, he noticed a pair of motorcycles rapidly approaching from behind. Seconds later, the two bikes roared up alongside the driver and passenger windows of his Volvo sedan — completely boxing him in.

Having navigated domestic disputes and gang interventions in his line of work, David knew the hallmarks of a planned attack when he saw one. The duo's tactics of pursuit and entrapment were clearly calculated.

His heart felt as though it was pounding in his chest. Yanking the steering wheel hard to the left, he slammed on the brakes, which sent his car skidding across the double yellow line as he desperately tried to break containment from his assailants.

The front fender of his Volvo collided with the driver's motorcycle with a nauseating crunch of metal, causing it to sway as it struggled to regain balance. Both bikes surged forward, blocking off any chance of escape. David was completely trapped with nowhere to go.

Instinctively hitting the gas again, he ploughed straight into the back of the trailing motorcycle, sending the rider somersaulting over the hood and windshield in a tangle of limbs before smashing onto the asphalt behind his car. For a split second, the instinct of being a doctor kicked in, and David slowed down, as he considered stopping to help.

However, he was rapidly brought back to the reality of what was happening when the lead motorcycle peeled off to the side, its rider dismounted and started to advance on David's car while holding an aluminium baseball bat. With adrenaline surging through his body, David knew it was now or never to make a break for it.

He floored the gas pedal, sending the car hurtling forward directly towards the rapidly approaching assailant. At the last second, the man tried diving out of the way, but it was too late. The solid thud and sickening crunch of the car's front bumper connecting with his leg shattered the tense quiet of the night.

David caught a glimpse in his rearview mirror of the man crumpled on the sidewalk, wailing in agony as he clutched his mangled leg. The shock of what just happened caused the colour to drain from David's face. He knew he had to flee as far as possible from these thugs before they regrouped and finished the job.

Peeling out, David floored the accelerator and tore through the suburban streets, his mind racing almost as fast as his battered car. Who were those two men? And more importantly — who had sent them after him?

The answer seemed evident, even if David couldn't yet substantiate it — somewhere during his investigation he must have hit a nerve. It could only be the individuals who felt threatened by his discoveries at Zooth Pharmaceuticals.

Self-perseverance and greed had obviously taken precedence, and as David dug deeper into Neuroloxyn. They obviously feared the truth about their deadly cash cow being made public and wanted to permanently shut down his investigation.

Just then, David's already frayed nerves were shattered by the sound of a thundering exhaust roaring up behind him. The first motorcycle was back and rapidly closing the distance to his car.

Looking in the sideview mirror, David watched in horror as the rider pulled up alongside him, continuing to match his speed with calm and terrifying precision. Then the man reached into his jacket with one hand, retrieving what appeared to be a sawn-off shotgun.

With reflexes born of pure survival instinct, David wrenched the steering wheel as hard as he could just as the masked rider opened fire. Twin blasts of gunfire erupted, immediately shattering the driver's side window with a deafening roar.

Ducking down as best he could, David felt a searing line of fire trace across his cheek as one of the projectiles grazed his neck. The piercing scream of the slug ricocheting into the dashboard filled the cramped cabin with a pungent haze of smoke and the smell of smouldering interior fabrics.

Peering through the blinding haze of shattered glass, David could see the motorcycle pulling ahead, clearly aiming to cut him off and finish the job at close quarters. A mile or so down the road, the rider stopped and turned around, before reloading his shotgun.

After several nerve-shattering revs, the motorcycle came racing towards David as though in a medieval joust. With a bone-dry mouth and his heart beating as though it were ready to explode, David gripped the steering wheel with grim determination.

With nerves of steel, he revved his Volvo's engine in retaliation and steadied his aim as the motorcycle drew closer and closer. Faced with a jousting charge, David had no alternative but to accept his challenge and take on his assailant head-on.

As the motorcycle closed in, the assassin raised his sawn-off shotgun and began to take aim. At the last possible second, and with a final rev of the engine, David tightened his jaw, cranked the wheel with every ounce of strength, and slammed the gas pedal to the floor. Two shotgun blasts echoed through the night air as the projectiles harmlessly slammed into the hood of the damaged Volvo.

The bone-crunching, high-speed impact of the car's heavy front end meeting the motorcycle head-to-head was catastrophic. David felt the Volvo's momentum shudder violently as the front suspension unloaded with the impact.

The motorcycle and its rider erupted into a twisting cyclone of metal and flesh, the roar of the engine cutting out in an instant as the man went rag-dolling twenty feet into the air from the sheer force of the collision.

Then...silence. David felt his chest heaving, his fingers clenched tightly around the steering wheel, knuckles turning white under the pressure as shock and adrenaline coursed through his veins.

In front of his shattered windshield, the twisted remains of the motorcycle lay burning in the middle of the empty street, illuminating the motionless body of its rider in a hellish backlight. The realisation of what just happened hit him like a freight train.

Had he actually killed the man, or was the motionless body in the road just severely injured? Either way, it was in self-defence. His racing heart told him he needed to flee the scene immediately before the other man or, heaven forbid, any other backup foot soldiers arrived to finish the job.

With trembling hands, he somehow managed to restart the damaged car and limp away, leaving a trail of debris and scattering sparks in his wake. His vision was swimming, shock setting in, but just a few miles ahead he saw the approaching glow of passing headlights on a main thoroughfare where he could find help...

David doesn't remember anything else from the night until waking up in the emergency ward of St. Joseph's Centre. It turned out a passer-by had found him slumped over in the driver's seat, barely conscious and bleeding in his badly damaged Volvo on the side of the road, his body battered and bruised.

Only after the drugs had worn off, did David fully comprehend how close he had come to being gruesomely murdered.

All because he was trying to do the right thing and expose the relentless truth about Neuroloxyn. The attempt on his life only confirmed his suspicions, inciting him to look deeper into the hidden secrets behind the drug. No matter how dark and perilous the path before him might become, he was not going to be deterred.

As David peeled off the bandages and took stock of his injuries in the mirror, he didn't feel the satisfaction of a man who had narrowly survived an assassination attempt. No, instead he felt a cold shiver of primal realisation shoot down his spine.

If it was Zooth Pharmaceuticals, and their goon squad behind the attempt on his life — they were playing for keeps. It meant that Jessica and him must have uncovered something far graver and more insidious than either of them could have anticipated. With deep pockets, money was no object for this large enterprise, and it now appeared that there were no lines they wouldn't cross to protect their billions in ill-gotten profits from Neuroloxyn's ongoing carnage around the globe.

If Jessica and David persisted in their quest for justice and accountability, they would surely not be so lucky next time. The next attack could come at any moment, in any form from a faceless hitman — and it would be utterly relentless until the job was done.

They had in no unmistaken terms, sent their most bone-chilling message, with those two motorcyclists — expose us at your own mortal peril. Drop this investigation or die.

A different Doctor might have wilted at that prospect. But David was no average Doctor and was not willing to be cowed by corporate muscle. He had been a decorated combat medic in Iraq and had witnessed the worst of human brutality and suffering first-hand on the battlefield.

He knew courage in the face of evil was always a simple choice — stand your ground, or step aside and enable further atrocities.

With halting steps, he made his way to the cramped bathroom attached to the ward. He needed a long, hot shower to wash away the final traces of the carnage before planning his next move.

As the scalding water pounded over his bruised face and shoulders, a look of cool determination reset his features. The gauntlet against Zooth Pharmaceuticals had now been thrown down in the most harrowing way imaginable — with literal bullets and spilt blood.

Fine, David thought to himself grimly, as the water swirled with his dried blood and grime down the drain. If these thugs wanted a war, he would not back down. Not after coming face-to-face with the depth of their depravity.

If Zooth's CEO, Gavin Caldwell, and his lieutenants wanted to kill the messenger and sweep their sins against humanity back under the rug of corporate criminality. Well, he would make sure that the rug was napalmed to ash, even if it meant sacrificing his life and future safety in the process.

Those responsible would pay their debt to society and the victims whose lives were cut short. The radiation of their guilt and deadly greed would be exposed for all to see before the entire world, providing a brutally overdue precedent of accountability for the pharmaceutical industry.

Shutting off the water, he stepped out and caught a glimpse of his battered reflection in the foggy mirror. A haunted visage stared back, but the eyes burned with a dark intensity born of a soul that had brushed against the grave only to emerge more resolute than ever before.

David made a solemn vow to never again rest until every last perpetrator involved with unleashing the Neuroloxyn catastrophe had faced the consequences their wanton cruelty deserved.

This was now a reckoning that would not be extinguished, no matter what other violence and depths of malice Zooth Pharmaceuticals was willing to sink to in pursuit of denying the inevitable and obscuring their guilt from the world in self-serving greed cloaked by corporate rhetoric.

David dried himself off, each motion of movement like a ritual of rebirth and hardening for the long battle that lay ahead. He would need to work quickly now that Zooth had revealed their willingness to have them eliminated at any price.

Dressing and packing up his meagre belongings, he cast one last look around the dingy hospital room that had nearly become his deathbed at the hands of corporate hitmen. Checking to ensure the hallway was clear, he stepped out and began walking with a noticeable limp towards the exit.

He still couldn't risk calling the police, not yet at least. Not until he rallied ironclad evidence and reinforcements against the veritable army that

Zooth's billions could muster to discredit or neutralise him.

With Jessica in his corner and the righteous fury driving him in the wake of his harrowing brush with death, David knew he now had the unshakable determination to expose the truth — no matter how far into the abyss of avarice and immorality he was forced to reach.

There would be no walking away now. Not when the promised riches and power of billions had driven Zooth to condone death and murder on a sickening scale, unseen in the corporate world.

David had stared into the darkest indifference of that all-consuming greed — and it had only strengthened his resolve to purge it from the planet with the ferocity of a man who had nothing left to lose.

Stepping out into the spring sunshine, he hailed a cab and headed to Emerald Harbour Medical Centre.

CHAPTER SEVEN

A Grim Reunion

THE YELLOW CAB inched forward in the snarling lunchtime traffic, exhaust fumes wafting into the stuffy interior. David stared out the window with a thousand-yard gaze, mentally attempting to process the whirlwind of events over the past twenty-four hours.

His world had been shattered in the most literal sense by the brutal assassination attempt that nearly claimed his life. He had spent a harrowing night drifting in and out of consciousness, each throbbing ache and searing flare of pain a visceral reminder of just how far Zooth Pharmaceuticals was willing to go to bury their secrets.

He had awoken in the hospital's emergency ward to find himself miraculously clinging to life, battered and bloodied but still breathing. After fleeing the facility to regroup with Jessica, he knew contacting the authorities would be useless at this stage. Not without the smoking gun evidence required to take down the impenetrable legal fortress of one of the world's largest drug companies.

Zooth Pharmaceuticals had revealed the demonic depths of their depravity with the bold assassination attempt. Any further pursuit by Jessica and him would clearly be met with even more extreme, unconscionable retaliation from their platoons of mercenary enforcers.

The one person whom he could trust to help validate his findings and possibly turn the tide was Jessica. His closest and most loyal colleague. The two of them had dug deep into the Zooth Pharmaceuticals investigation, leaving no stone unturned.

Jessica had been poring over medical databases and autopsy logs in parallel with David, aghast at the mounting evidence of Neuroloxyn's side effects. But, even she was unaware of just how far their research had ventured into the rabbit hole of Zooth's criminality. They had apparently ventured close enough to stare into the bloody maw of the beast and earn a death mark for their dogged persistence.

When Jessica arrived at the hospital, David was nowhere to be seen. By midday, when he had failed to show up for work, a fresh jolt of adrenaline and dread coursed through her veins. Her gut began twisting itself into knots, fearing the worst. It was not like him to go radio silent without any word. Had something happened to him? Calling his mobile it went straight to voice mail.

Had Zooth's hatchet men done something to cause him to disappear off the face of the earth?

Those grave thoughts soon dissipated as she spotted his haggard silhouette emerging from the yellow cab. Never in her life had Jessica felt such relief and bone-deep gratitude as when David limped towards her, a bleary but determined look in his eyes. Rushing forward, she embraced him in a fierce bear hug, unmindful of the stares from bystanders all around the medical plaza.

"Oh my god," she sobbed into his shoulder. "I thought...I thought they had..." Jessica trailed off, unable to complete the anguished thought out loud as the emotions cascaded over her.

David patted her back with a wince, separating from the hug just enough so she could see the raw scratches, mottled bruising, and hastily applied bandages covering his face and neck. A ghastly reminder of the abject savagery he had suffered at the hands of Zooth Pharmaceuticals remorseless butchers.

Jessica clasped her hands over her mouth in horror at his brutalised appearance. "Dear god, David...they really did try to kill you!"

David nodded wearily, the icy glint of animalistic fury entering his eyes like memorialised trauma. "Oh yeah — those Zooth fuckers sent their very best enforcers after me. And they made absolutely sure I got the message."

The gruesome details of his story had Jessica's stomach churning with nausea. She fought back the urge to retch as David flatly recounted how the two motorcycle assassins had ambushed him in the street, boxed his car in, and systematically attempted to execute him.

Only his sharpened survival instincts, honed from years of battlefront triage work as a military medic, had enabled him to evade their initial attacks in a desperate escape bid. Even then, in the final harrowing moments before blacking out from blood loss and shock, he'd had the burst of clarity and foresight to ram his vehicle into the second shooter in a kamikaze manoeuvre that likely saved his life.

"But not before he got these little souvenirs..." He tenderly touched the fresh line of stitches running along his neck.

Jessica shuddered, wondering just how close her friend and colleague had come to being murdered in cold blood by the forces of human evil and rapacious greed. As if Zooth Pharmaceuticals wasn't already damned enough in her mind for their mercenary role in propagating the Neuroloxyn scandal, now they had crossed the unthinkable line of explicitly trying to eliminate truth-tellers through brutal violence.

"So, what now?" ...she asked David quietly, unconsciously glancing around the crowded outdoor plaza for any sign of impending ambush. The toll this investigation was extracting, just kept getting steeper and steeper. "Please tell me you have a plan?"

"Yes," he replied flatly.

"We go off the grid, I can't take the risk of trying to chase leads or paperwork any longer, not after they so brazenly marked me for elimination."

David grimaced and flexed his hand, sending spasms of pain lancing through still-healing bones. "But I'm done running from these sick fucks and their billions. It's time we finally fought back, hard

— with any means necessary."

He unconsciously brushed the old Army field jacket he was wearing, the same tattered garment she'd seen him throw on a thousand times for late nights interrogating datasets at odd hours. Only now, it seemed imbued with preternatural symbolic power as the mantle for a very different kind of urban warfare.

"Starting from square one, we go through everything we have. We have unknowingly stumbled across something that they are afraid will get out. We're going to build an ironclad case leveraging every scrap of evidence amassed so far," he continued darkly. "And once we have the Zooth demons nailed shut in a coffin of hard proof, we'll rain hellfire from every direction. Criminal charges, Senate hearings, whistleblower lawsuits — the whole nine yards. I want to see that poisonous company's wealth and very existence salted from the face of the Earth."

"Okay," … Jessica swallowed hard and gave a decisive nod. "Let's get started. We've got a war to win."

CHAPTER EIGHT

Descent into the Abyss

THE DINGY MOTEL room's cramped confines were barely visible through the towers of boxes filled with medical files, studies, and reams of printouts strewn in an almost archaeological sprawl covering every flat surface.

Jessica, her eyes strained and burning with fatigue, squinted at her monitor as she sifted through medical journal articles for what felt like the umpteenth time. A half-eaten burger lay congealing next to her keyboard as she made yet another pass through the data maze.

Looking up expectantly from the stack of manila file folders piled in his lap, David asked, "Anything?"

Jessica shook her head wearily. "Nothing new jumping out so far from this Rutgers paper, but we can definitely correlate their data on cardiac side effects with at least a dozen more cases in our files."

She massaged her temples, trying to dispel the migraine pounding behind her eyes. For two straight weeks now, they had been living out of this fleabag hideout strategically chosen for its remote location and scant traffic. A haven from prying eyes where amidst the anonymity of peeling wallpaper and flickering fluorescent lights, they could comb through their trove of archived materials undisturbed and search for any missing pieces.

The demonic puzzle's endgame was finally starting to take shape, though it's terrifying outlines raised more nightmarish questions than concrete answers about Zooth Pharmaceuticals' true culpability in the Neuroloxyn disaster. What they'd uncovered lurking behind the clinical veneer of data so far seemed to border on not just gross negligence, but outright conspiracy to commit premeditated fraud in exchange for profit.

David growled and tossed another folder down in frustration. "I'm telling you Jess, this goes all the way to the damn top at Zooth Pharmaceuticals'. My gut says Caldwell and his C-suite hatchet men knew Neuroloxyn's risks from day one, and made an intentional and wilful decision to roll the dice on public safety."

Not for the first time, as he idly touched the ropy pink scar snaking along his neck from being grazed by an assassin's bullet. A haunting souvenir of just how psychopathically far Zooth Pharmaceuticals management would go to bury any truths threatening their bottom line.

"The more we dig, the more it stinks of a massive cover-up preying on compartmentalisation and God knows how much regulatory corruption. They must have had compromised FDA medical officers from the start on the payroll to bless Neuroloxyn's approvals while cooking the books." David raged, pinching the bridge of his nose in exasperation.

Jessica nodded grimly, all too familiar with the rot

of embedded institutional cronyism that allowed corporate players to exploit regulatory loopholes and rubber-stamp practices with little more than a wink and greased palms. They had both witnessed far too many instances of it during their medical careers.

But never anything on the catastrophic, apocalyptic scale of negligence and premeditation that Zooth Pharmaceuticals seemed to be guilty of. A poisoned dagger had been plunged directly into the heart of the American public health system, all in the cynical pursuit of sales targets and shareholder value.

"Well, we know Neuroloxyn was rushed through preliminary clinical trials and fast-tracked against the FDA's own guidelines," Jessica replied, erasing the database queries polluting her laptop screen before reopening a fresh window. "What we still haven't confirmed is just how deep employee concerns over dodgy safety data went — and how far up the chain that intel made it to Zooth Pharmaceuticals C-suite."

She paused, her face hardening with renewed determination. "Somewhere in these Goddamned boxes, we have to find the documentation laying it all out — how their entire pharmaceutical machine wilfully ignored years of red flags and lethal side effects, all because Neuroloxyn profit projections blinded them to basic human decency."

With a heavy sigh, Jessica pushed back from her

laptop and rose stiffly from the hard motel chair that had become a semi-permanent workstation.

"I'm ordering some fresh hard drives and burner laptops from a speciality shop two cities over," she announced, stretching out cramped muscles. "If, or rather when, we manage to unearth all the evidence for our case – I want it organised and backed up in triplicate on multiple secure mobile rigs. Just in case..."

She trailed off, not needing to verbalise the darker implications. If – no, when – Zooth Pharmaceuticals caught wind that the final noose was tightening around their collective necks, they would no doubt renew efforts to neutralise any whistleblowers with extreme prejudice.

"Good call on the backup hardware," David nodded approvingly. "We'll need to be able to mobilise and disappear with everything at a moment's notice."

CHAPTER NINE

The Mourning After

THE PIERCING RING of Jessica's phone shattered the stillness of the room. Her hand instinctively darted out to grab it, heart quickening with unease as she saw Dr Michael's Bennett's name and number flashing on the screen. A knot twisted in her stomach — he wouldn't be calling at this hour unless it was gravely important.

Curiosity mingled with apprehension as Jessica answered the call. "Hello? Michael, what's going on? Is everything okay?"

"Good morning Jess," his voice trembled with sorrow, " I didn't want you to hear it from anyone else, I'm sorry to be the bearer of bad news, but it's Ethan. We...we tried everything, but his cognitive decline was too much. He finally succumbed to it last night. I'm so sorry. I know what he meant to you."

Jessica felt her world tilt violently on its axis as the weight of Michael's words came crashing down. Tears welled in her eyes, a lump forming in her throat as the news fully registered.

The once cheerful and energetic twelve-year-old, had become shrouded in mystery. His vibrant life had taken a dark turn, and now he was gone. A promising young life, brilliant beyond his years, had been claimed far too soon. The very medicine intended to heal him had instead become his undoing, ravaging his body until there was nothing left.

"Oh my god..." she gasped, struggling to maintain composure as visceral grief swept over her. Jessica managed to muster a heartfelt thank you before concluding the conversation. "Th...thank you for letting me know, Michael. I ...I appreciate you calling."

But as soon as she hung up, the dam burst. Great heaving sobs wracked her body as the full brunt of Ethan's tragic fate washed over her.

From across the dimly lit room, David looked up in alarm at his friend and partner's anguished cries. Without a moment's hesitation, he shot up and rushed over, putting a supportive arm around Jessica's shuddering shoulders.

"Jess? Jess, what's going on? Are you okay?" he asked urgently, trying to coax her to make eye contact while simultaneously surveying for any sign of external threat.

"Th...that was Michael," Jessica managed between wracking gasps of air. "It's E...Ethan. He's...he's gone. David, the damage Neuroloxyn did to his brain finally killed him."

She dissolved back into sobs, clutching her face in her hands as if trying to physically contort away from the emotional torment. David felt his heart plummet into his gut as the news of Ethan's passing settled heavily, a young schoolboy silenced prematurely. Ethan was robbed of the opportunity to walk across the graduation stage.

Ethan's life, and those of thousands more duped into using the poison called Neuroloxyn, had been sacrificed at the altar of institutional greed and criminality.

"Aw Jess, I...I'm so sorry," David uttered, his voice catching slightly as he pulled Jessica in for a fierce embrace. He stroked her hair, buying the emotion welling up behind his own eyes as the interminable price of their crusade resonated. "I know how much Ethan meant to you, to all of us really. God, this entire nightmare just feels...totally senseless all over again."

For several long moments, the two doctors clung to each other, drawing what comfort they could as fresh mourning breeze washed over the room.

This tragic vignette was the raw face of corporate criminality's homicidal wake that could never be reversed or rationalised through empty apologies, however begrudgingly rendered. Loved ones, human beings with loves, dreams and entire worlds of emotional dimensionality snuffed out for the most callow of motivations.

As her sobs began subsiding into wet hiccups, David slowly pulled away from their embrace, gazing intently at Jessica's haunted features with a protective big brother's stare.

"Listen Jess...I know this is absolutely gutting in every possible way," he murmured carefully. "But I need you to really hear me now, okay? We can't let Ethan's sacrifice, or the thousands of others who never got their day in court to achieve this justice — we can't let it get diminished or forgotten with the passage of time."

Jessica sniffled hard, composing herself enough to appreciate the gravity of David's words.

"I'm with you David. I understand," she replied, almost startling herself with the eerie steadiness returning to her voice. "We have to see this through to the very end now. It's the only way Ethan's tragedy, all of their ordeals, don't get overshadowed or lost amid the next outrage cycle. We owe them that commitment"

David squeezed her shoulder firmly, flashing a proud, resolute grin in the face of such shared conviction rekindled from the ashes.

"That's the spirit, partner. For Ethan's sake, for all the victims, we keep swinging our sword until permanent systemic reforms are chiselled in bedrock. Only then can we maybe start healing from all the suffering these soulless bastards inflicted."

"You got it," Jessica replied, the fire of determination smouldering with renewed vigour behind her watery eyes. "Let's get back to work dismantling their whole damned citadel and showing the world how deep this plague of corporate butchery goes. No holding back, no more pulling punches."

As David and Jessica systematically sifted through a never-ending pile of patient files, David fumed with fresh fervour while Jessica channelled her anguish into laser-focused intensity. A solemn pact reverberated between them: the demons of capitalist ruthlessness that had claimed so many martyrs like Ethan would never truly rest, necessitating an equally relentless vanguard to beat back the darkness in perpetuity.

It was their vigil to bear now, with the truth's light upheld and shining eternally whatever loved ones and casualties became burdened along that scorched path. For the lost voices could never be truly silenced so long as those bearing ethical witness persisted in shouting their mortal echoes.

CHAPTER TEN

The Whistleblower

THE WEIGHT OF their crusade against Zooth Pharmaceuticals and the insidious reach of Neuroloxyn seemed to grow heavier with each passing day, a burden that threatened to crush even the most resolute of souls.

Amid this gathering storm, a glimmer of hope emerged, a ray of light that pierced the darkness and reignited the fires of determination within Jessica and David.

It began with a phone call, the shrilling ring cutting through the tense silence of the dingy motel's room like a clarion call. Jessica reached for her mobile, her brow furrowed with a mixture of trepidation and curiosity at the unidentified number.

Every ring sent shivers down her spine, each one a deafening reminder of the potential danger lurking on the other end. With each shrilling ring, her heart pounded harder, echoing the unavoidable fear that gripped her soul and exposed her to the ominous tentacles of Zooth Pharmaceuticals. With trembling hands, she answered the phone, her weary voice barely able to muster a response.

"Hello,"

"Hello...Dr McClain," a voice murmured on the other end, the words laced with a sense of urgency that sent a shiver down her spine.

"Speaking," Jessica replied, her fingers tightening around the mobile, as a sense of foreboding washed over her.

"I don't have much time," the voice continued, the words tumbling out in a rushed whisper. "I'm a pharmacist at Zooth Pharmaceuticals, and I can't stay silent any longer."

Jessica's heart raced as the implications of the caller's words sank in. Is this the long-awaited breakthrough they've been looking for, the missing piece of the puzzle that would unravel the web of deceit surrounding Neuroloxyn?

"Go on," she urged, her voice barely above a whisper.

"I was part of the team that developed Neuroloxyn," the voice pressed on, a tremor of fear threading through the words. "From the beginning, there were concerns about potentially dangerous side effects, but the higher-ups insisted on pushing forward."

A surge of righteous indignation coursed through Jessica's veins as she listened to the pharmacist's account. It was a tale she had heard far too often, a tragic refrain that echoed throughout the annals of corporate greed and disregard for human life.

"We tried to sound the alarm," the voice continued, "but our warnings fell on deaf ears. The executives were blinded by the promise of profits, and they were willing to sacrifice patient safety in pursuit of their goals."

Jessica's grip tightened around her mobile as she processed the gravity of the pharmacist's revelations. It was one thing to suspect corporate malfeasance, but to have it confirmed by a so-called insider, was a game-changer, a bombshell that threatened to shatter the carefully constructed façade of Zooth Pharmaceuticals public image.

A haunting question, however, lingered in Jessica: who was this mysterious caller? Their identity remained cloaked in a shadow of darkness, as they refused to reveal themselves, leaving her to grapple with the chilling realisation that danger could be lurking on the other end. Was it the malevolent hand of Zooth, weaving a web of deception to manipulate the course of her investigation? Or perhaps a shadowy figure fuelled by a burning vendetta against Zooth Pharmaceuticals, ready to unleash havoc?

With every unanswered question, Jessica's hardened determination ignited like a flame in the night. But she knew one thing for certain: she needed tangible proof, a beacon of truth to pierce through the veil of uncertainty and guide her through the darkness.

"That's not all," the voice pressed on, the words laced with a sense of urgency that sent a shiver down Jessica's spine. "There were rumours, whispers of bribery and corruption at the highest levels."

Jessica's breath caught in her throat as the pharmacist's words sank in. Could it be possible that the tentacles of Zooth Pharmaceuticals' deceit had reached into the very halls of the regulatory bodies meant to protect the public?

"There was talk of an official at the FDA being paid off," the voice hissed, the words barely audible over the crackle of the phone line. "A man named Richard Barkly. He was instrumental in pushing Neuroloxyn through the approval process, despite the mounting evidence of potential risks."

Jessica felt a surge of adrenaline coursing through her veins as the pieces of the puzzle began to fall into place. This was the flaming revelation she was looking for.

Richard Barkly – a name she had come across in her research, a name that those who dared to question the FDA's decisions had whispered in hushed tones.

"You need to investigate this," the voice urged, a sense of desperation creeping into his words, " Barkly is the key to unravelling this whole sordid affair. But be careful, Dr McClain. These people are dangerous and will stop at nothing to protect their interests."

With those ominous words, the line went dead, leaving Jessica reeling in the wake of the pharmacist's revelations. She sat frozen, her mobile clutched in her trembling hand, her mind racing with the implications of what she had just heard. It was a game-changer, a bombshell that threatened to blow the lid off one of the most insidious scandals to rock the pharmaceutical industry in decades. But with that revelation came a sense of dread, a palpable awareness of the forces arrayed against them and the lengths to which Zooth Pharmaceuticals would go to protect their interests.

Pale as a ghost, Jessica's gaping maw sent shivers down David's spine as she gazed into the abyss. "Jessica, what... what just happened?" David's voice quivered with concern. "What was that all about?"

Wasting no time, she recounted the pharmacist's shocking revelations, her words pouring out to unravel the unfathomable. With the realisation of what just happened, David's mind went into overdrive.

"This... this changes everything Jess," David breathed a sigh of relief, his words were laced with a mixture of disbelief and determination. "If what this whistleblower is saying is true, we're dealing with a level of corruption that goes far beyond anything we could have imagined."

Jessica nodded; her jaw set in a grim line. "We need to investigate this Richard Barkly, dig into his past, his connections, and his dealings with Zooth Pharmaceuticals. If he truly is the linchpin in this whole sordid affair, then exposing him could be the key to unravelling the entire conspiracy."

A heavy silence hung between them, punctuated only by the rhythmic tapping of David's fingers against the table. They both knew the risks and the dangers that lay ahead, but they also knew that there was no turning back — not now, not when they were so close to the truth.

"We'll need to move quickly and discreetly," David said finally, his voice laced with a sense of urgency. "Zooth Pharmaceuticals will have eyes and ears everywhere, and if they catch wind of our investigation into Barkly, they'll do everything in their power to shut us down."

Jessica confirmed David's thoughts, her mind already formulating a plan of action. "I'll reach out to our network and see if anyone has any leads or information on Richard Barkly's activities. We must construct a solid case, capable of enduring the scrutiny of both the courts and the media.

With the echoing of those words, the gears of change started to shift, marking the beginning of a new era in their battle against Zooth Pharmaceuticals. No longer were they merely fighting against a pharmaceutical behemoth; they now stood as warriors challenging a labyrinthine network of corruption and avarice, a system so deeply rooted that it had insidiously seeped into the very veins of institutions designed to safeguard the public.

In the days and weeks that followed, Jessica and David worked tirelessly, sifting through mountains of data and consulting with a vast network of allies. They traced Richard Barkly's movements, his connections, and his dealings with Zooth Pharmaceuticals, piecing together a damning portrait of corruption and betrayal.

As the evidence mounted, so too did the sense of urgency and the ever-present spectre of danger. Threats and intimidation tactics became commonplace, with anonymous messages and ominous warnings arriving at all hours of the day and night.

Jessica and David remained resolute, their determination fuelled by a burning sense of righteous indignation and a steadfast belief in the principles that had drawn them to the medical profession.

They were well aware that they were playing a dangerous game, one that pitted them against forces far more powerful and well-resourced than they could ever hope to be. But in their hearts, they carried a conviction that transcended the boundaries of their safety — a conviction that the truth must be brought to light, no matter the cost.

As the noose tightened around Richard Barkly and the intricate web of corruption shielding Zooth Pharmaceuticals' misdeeds, Jessica and David found themselves teetering on the edge of a monumental confrontation. It wasn't just about their careers anymore; it was about upholding the integrity of the pharmaceutical industry itself.

Once mere doctors advocating for their patients,

they now bore the weight of a crosshair squarely on their backs. They had shed their white coats to don the armour of warriors, battling against the relentless onslaught of corporate greed and deception. This was more than a fight for justice; it was a battle for the very soul of medicine itself.

In this treacherous terrain, trust became a luxury they could ill afford; every step had to be calculated, every action scrutinised. Yet, undeterred by the looming shadows of doubt, they pressed forward with unwavering determination. They were not just seeking victory; they were fighting to reclaim the essence of healing in a world where it had been dangerously tarnished.

They knew that the road ahead would be fraught with peril; armed with the knowledge of their cause, they were prepared to face it head-on.

CHAPTER ELEVEN

The Darkest Hour

THE RADIO CRACKLED with static, as the newscaster's voice cut through the tense silence that had enveloped the dingy room. As the details of an unidentified man's death spilt forth, "…an unidentified victim's vehicle has been discovered at the base of a ravine, its wreckage indicating a severe loss of control. Authorities are investigating the incident as a possible homicide, given the presence of suspicious evidence at the scene."

The newscaster continued "…investigators discovered an access card in the possession of the deceased, and it is believed that the victim was an employee of Zooth Pharmaceuticals." Jessica and David turned to each other as a chill ran down their spines, an ominous premonition that threatened to shatter the fragile resolve they had so carefully cultivated.

"If anyone has information that could aid in the identification of the victim or the circumstances surrounding his death, they are asked to urgently contact Detective Stables of the Seattle Police Department."

Jessica's knuckles whitened as she gripped the arms of her chair, her mind racing with the implications of the newscaster's words. Could it be a mere coincidence? Or was this the grim fate that awaited those who dared to challenge the might of Zooth Pharmaceuticals?

The air seemed to grow thick with tension, the weight of the revelations bearing down upon them like a physical force. They had known the risks when going in and had steeled themselves for the possibility of retaliation. But even after the attempt on David's life, nothing could have prepared them for the stark reality of taking the life of a whistleblower in pursuit of the truth.

As the news report faded into the background, Jessica's mind raced, piecing together the fragments of information that had been laid before her. An unidentified victim, the Zooth Pharmaceuticals access card, the suspicious nature of the accident — it all pointed to a grim coincidence, one that sent a shockwave of fear rippling through her very being.

Could this be the pharmacist who had reached out to her just days earlier, the brave soul who had risked everything to shed light on the corruption festering within the halls of Zooth Pharmaceuticals? The thought sent a chill down her spine, a sobering reminder of the depths to which their adversaries were willing to sink to protect their interests.

With trembling hands, and her mind a whirlwind of emotions — fear, outrage, and a burning determination that threatened to consume her from within. She turned to face David.

"David," she said, her voice laced with a mixture of trepidation and resolve. "Did you hear that? It's bad."

There was a pause, a pregnant silence that seemed to stretch into eternity. Then, David muttered in disbelief.

"I know, I heard it," he said, his words laced with a heaviness that spoke volumes. "If it's who we think it is..."

Jessica nodded. "Then we're dealing with forces far more dangerous than we ever could have imagined."

Another pause, punctuated only by the rhythmic tapping of David's fingers against the table — a nervous tic that betrayed the gravity of the situation.

"We can't back down now Jess," he said finally, his voice steeled with a resolve that seemed to belie the weight of the circumstances. "If they're willing to go to such lengths to silence a whistleblower, it only underscores the importance of what we're doing."

Jessica took a deep breath, steadying herself against the onslaught of emotions that threatened to overwhelm her. She knew David was right — they had come too far, sacrificed too much, to let fear and intimidation deter them from their path.

"You're right," she said, her voice growing stronger with each syllable. "We press on, but we need to be smarter, and more cautious. These people are not playing, they have shown that they are willing to play by their own set of rules, and we can't afford to underestimate them."

David's assent was a quiet affirmation, a tacit acknowledgement of the perilous road that lay before them. They were no longer simply battling a pharmaceutical giant; they were waging war against a deeply entrenched system of corruption and deceit.

Jessica found herself grappling with a newfound sense of vulnerability. The sanctity of their cause had been shattered, replaced by a harsh reality where the lines between right and wrong had become dangerously blurred.

A realisation then dawned upon her, a glimmer of hope amidst the gathering darkness. To stand any hope of unveiling the truth and ensuring that the perpetrators face consequences, they would need to enlist the aid of allies beyond the confines of the medical community.

**

With a renewed sense of purpose, Jessica set her sights on the media — the watchdogs of democracy, the guardians of truth and transparency. She knew that the road ahead would be fraught with challenges, but she also knew that the power of the press could be a formidable weapon in their arsenal.

In the days that followed, Jessica and David reached out to their network of contacts, casting a wide net in search of journalists and media outlets willing to take on the daunting task of exposing the Zooth Pharmaceuticals scandal.

Their efforts were met with a mixture of scepticism and cautious interest, as the journalists they approached grappled with the weight of the allegations and the potential repercussions of taking on such a powerful adversary.

Yet, amidst the sea of hesitation, a beacon of hope emerged in the form of Amelia Sinclair, a renowned investigative reporter with a reputation for fearlessness and an unwavering commitment to the truth.

From the moment Jessica and David laid out the evidence before her, Amelia's eyes burned with a fierce determination, a hunger to unravel the tangled web of deceit and bring the perpetrators to justice.

"This is huge, it's bigger than what I had imagined," Amelia said, her voice laced with a sense of awe and trepidation. "If what you're saying is true, we're dealing with a level of corruption that strikes at the very heart of our society's trust in the institutions meant to protect us."

Jessica nodded; her gaze unwavering. "That's why we need your help Amelia. We've exhausted every avenue within the medical community, and now it's time to take this fight to the public arena."

Amelia's brow furrowed as she sifted through the evidence before her, her mind already formulating the framework of an exposé that would rock the foundations of the pharmaceutical industry.

"This won't be easy," she cautioned, her eyes meeting Jessica's with a steely resolve. "Zooth Pharmaceuticals has deep pockets and powerful allies. They'll throw everything they have at us in an attempt to discredit our story and bury the truth."

David leaned forward, his expression grim. "We're aware of the risks Amelia. But we've come too far, sacrificed too much, to back down now. The lives of countless patients hang in the balance, and we owe it to them to see this through to the bitter end."

Amelia nodded; her jaw set in a determined line. "Then we move forward, and we move forward with everything we've got. No stone is to be left unturned; no avenue unexplored. We'll shine a light on the darkest corners of this conspiracy, and we'll let the truth be our guiding beacon."

***

A new chapter began to unfold in their crusade against Zooth Pharmaceuticals. Jessica and David found themselves working in tandem with Amelia and her team of seasoned journalists, pooling their resources and expertise in a concerted effort to unravel the tangled web of deceit.

As the investigation deepened, the stakes grew higher, and the threats more palpable. Anonymous messages and ominous warnings continued to flood in, each one a grim reminder of the forces arrayed against them.

Armed with the knowledge that their cause was just and their resolve unshakable, a battle raged in the shadows of their minds. Jessica, David, and Amelia were determined to be the ones to emerge victorious, the beacons of hope in a world where the lines between healing and harm, truth and falsehood, and life and death, had become dangerously blurred.

As the investigation reached a fever pitch, the weight of their responsibility grew heavier with each passing day. They were fighting for the very fabric of trust that held society together, a trust that had been eroded by the insidious machinations of those who valued profits over human lives.

In their darkest moments, when the path ahead seemed shrouded in uncertainty and the forces arrayed against them seemed insurmountable, they found comfort in the knowledge that they were not alone.

For in their ranks were allies, kindred spirits who had been drawn to the cause by a shared sense of outrage and a burning desire to see justice prevail. These allies came from all walks of life — doctors, nurses, researchers, families of those deceased and even former employees of Zooth Pharmaceuticals. Employees who could no longer stay silent, they had witnessed the corruption first-hand and were previously too scared to speak out in lure of the ramifications.

Together, they formed an unbreakable chain, a bulwark against the tide of deceit and greed that threatened to sweep them away. Standing shoulder to shoulder, their ranks swelled by the righteous and the brave, they knew that they were part of something larger than themselves — a movement that transcended the boundaries of profession and circumstance, united in a common pursuit of truth and accountability.

As the world watched on helplessly, the devastation of Neuroloxyn was casting in its wake, Jessica, David, Amelia, and their allies prepared to unleash the bombshell that would shake the foundations of the pharmaceutical industry. They had amassed a mountain of evidence, a damning indictment of the corruption that had taken root within the halls of Zooth Pharmaceuticals and the regulatory bodies that were meant to safeguard the public trust.

And in the eye of this gathering storm, they stood tall, their resolve tempered by the sacrifices they had endured and the knowledge that their fight was not just for themselves, but for the countless victims whose lives had been forever altered by the pursuit of greed.

Prepared to take their stand, they did so with the knowledge that they were more than just individuals; they were champions, warriors in a war for the very soul of the medical profession and the integrity of the institutions meant to protect and serve.

The road ahead would be fraught with obstacles and dangers, but they were ready to face the tempest head-on, armed with the unwavering conviction that justice would ultimately prevail.

***

The dim shadows of the Media House's parking garage provided the perfect ambush for Zooth's merciless enforcers to strike. As Amelia made her way to her car, three figures appeared from the shadows. Amelia found herself surrounded by a pack of snarling brutes. Their demands were as blunt as they clutched their brass knuckles in their meaty fists — "Stop your investigation now. If you reveal what evidence you think you have, you will suffer the unbearable consequences."

To her immense credit, Sinclair displayed a bravery that belied her slight frame, defiantly refusing to be cowed by their vicious threats and violent attempts at intimidation. When their strong-arming tactics failed to break her unyielding resolve, the sadistic pack recognised the need for still direr measures to silence her.

With a nauseating flurry, they launched a sickening attack on Sinclair's larynx, desperately seeking to crush her voice before she could expose their nefarious sins to the world.

When news of Amelia's attack reached Jessica and David, they were horrified at the violence Zooth was prepared to inflict and decided to contact the authorities.

David felt a knot forming in the pit of his stomach as he ended the call with the Seattle Police Department. He had expected them to take his allegations about Zooth Pharmaceuticals more seriously, but instead, he was being passed off to the Feds. A stark reminder of just how big this could be.

David spoke with Special Agent Marcus Thorne of the FBI's healthcare fraud task force. Thorne had been brusque but professional on the phone. The FBI had been investigating Zooth Pharmaceuticals for over a year already, building a case around the systematic concealment of life-threatening side effects of their drugs. When David explained that he, along with Dr McClain and renowned investigative reporter, Amelia Sinclair, had amassed a substantial cache of insider evidence exposing Zooth's deliberate concealment of Neuroloxyn's deadly side effects, Thorne's interest was piqued, revealing an intense hunger for the kind of smoking gun that could blast this case wide open.

But he had also issued a firm warning, "Going public now could jeopardise the Bureau's case and allow Zooth Pharmaceuticals top brass to bury the trail, they had been working so hard on.' Thorne wanted to review their evidence first to see if it could buttress the FBI's case or potentially blow it wide open. He booked a flight from Miami to Seattle.

David turned to Jessica and Amelia and saw the same mixture of anticipation and dread mirrored on their faces. They had come too far to back out now, but crossing the FBI could land them in seriously hot water.

"Well, you heard the man," Jessica said finally. "We prepare everything for presentation and pray we have that 'smoking gun' he needs."

Over the next two days, they meticulously organised all the evidence they had painstakingly collected over months of secret efforts. Patient files, autopsy reports, Leaked emails, documenting in chilling detail how Zooth Pharmaceuticals had systemically buried reports of Neuroloxyn's life-threatening side effects and internal memos instructing researchers to alter haematological data. Included was a harrowing paper trail of colleagues who had died or committed suicide after raising concerns about the drug's safety.

It painted a deeply disturbing picture of a pharmaceutical juggernaut that had allowed greed to trample all ethical boundaries, willingly gambling with people's lives in pursuit of profit.

But would it be enough? Did they have the smoking gun that the FBI was looking for?

CHAPTER TWELVE

Raising the Stakes

DRUMMING HIS FINGERS against the steering wheel, Special Agent Marcus Thorne sat in tense silence, his unmarked sedan idling in the gloom of the parking garage. His gaze darting between his wristwatch and the entrance to the abandoned office building where he was supposed to meet his new informants.

At 42 years old, Thorne was one of the rising stars in the FBI's Miami field office. He cut an imposing figure with a stocky build, close-cropped hair, and the permanent serious expression of someone who had seen too many of life's harsh realities up close.

For the past 18 months, Thorne had been spearheading the Bureau's investigation into Zooth Pharmaceuticals - codenamed CROSSBONE. What had started as a routine inquiry into possible Medicare fraud had quickly spiralled into something exponentially more serious.

As the special agent in charge, Thorne had overseen a multi-jurisdictional task force compiling evidence that the massive drug company had wilfully overlooked clinical data showing that its blockbuster drug Neuroloxyn had potentially fatal side effects. All in pursuit of rushing the medication through approvals and getting it on the market before any competitors could mount a challenge.

It was yet another sickening case study of corporate greed, costing thousands of lives just to satisfy Wall Street projections and earn senior executives their performance bonuses. But nailing a behemoth like Zooth meant producing the undeniable smoking gun - something the Bureau had yet to obtain despite raids and exhaustive document analysis.

That was until Thorne received a frantic encrypted call three days ago from Dr David Reynolds, who claimed to possess the Holy Grail of incriminating data and testimony the Feds had been chasing. After some hushed back-and-forth, Thorne had demanded an in-person delivery before considering any evidenced-based courses of action.

Which was how he now found himself parked in this subterranean garage straight out of a spy movie, thrumming with nervous energy. Could Dr Reynolds and his two accomplices actually be the breakthrough the CROSSBONE task force so desperately needed? Or were they just another trio of well-intentioned wing-nuts chasing shadows and internet conspiracy theories?

Thorne scowled, chewing on the ragged stub of an unlit cigar out of pure nervous habit. He detested these freelance whistleblower types who always seemed to muck up legitimate investigations in search of their own brand of justice. More often than not, they ended up doing more harm than good with reckless behaviour that got them hurt or compromised an FBI ironclad case.

Still, there had been an unmistakable urgency in Dr Reynolds' voice. The man had claimed he and his team were sitting on a mountain of damning internal communications directly tying Zooth Pharmaceuticals' criminal practices to its C-suite exec committee. They even had credible threats of violence made against Dr Reynolds and his crew, purportedly from the pharmaceutical giant's own hired security teams.

Thorne snorted, adjusting his tie. What company deployed Corporate Assassin Squad-level containment teams to deal with some rabble-rousing academics? This whole situation stank of amateur-hour bravado mixed with outright delusion. Yet his finely tuned investigator's Spidey senses told him to at least hear Dr Reynolds out in person.

His rumination's were interrupted as a dented black Camry pulled into the garage, headlights scanning the concrete before jerking to a halt. Thorne watched warily as three figures emerged from the vehicle, approaching with caution as if any sudden moves might startle him.

Dr Reynolds was immediately recognisable, his scarred face still bearing the pinkish weal from whatever violence he claimed to have survived. Flanking him were two women, both in their mid-thirties - one with close-cropped auburn hair in a simple white blouse and khakis, the other a trim Asian-American wearing a powder-blue sundress.

"Special Agent Thorne?" Reynolds asked once the trio drew close enough.

"That's me," Thorne replied evenly, already sizing up the two women and evaluating potential threat levels. "You're Dr Reynolds and these are your compatriots, McClain and Sinclair, I take it? The whistleblower Doctors trying to get the 60 Minutes expose every starry-eyed brand spanking new ADA thinks will set the world on fire?"

He didn't bother masking his scepticism. Leading with gruff dismissiveness was Thorne's trademark tactic for sifting the bullshit artists from anyone operating on the level.

Amelia shot him a look of open irritation at his derisive tone, but Dr Reynolds quickly stepped forward with an upraised palm to defuse the tension.

"Fair enough to be dubious Agent. We know our reputations probably precede us as The Crusaders desperate to take down Big Pharma. But the intel package we're offering is comprehensive enough to make true believers out of the biggest cynics in your ranks, I promise you that."

Now it was Thorne's turn to look askance. The resolve and intensity burning behind Dr Reynolds' eyes was unmistakable. Whatever had put that look there, the agent knew he was dealing with someone tempered by trauma and injustice on a searing visceral level.

Almost against his will, Thorne found himself wanting to at least scroll through the purported evidence this man was so adamant about providing. With a grunt of concession, he popped the trunk on his unmarked sedan and motioned for Dr Reynolds and his crew to stow whatever data they had brought with them.

Dr McClain stepped forward, hoisting a weathered satchel loaded with external hard drives and burner laptops that clanged loudly when she set it down in the trunk's well.

"Here's the entire repository, everything we've compiled and archived over the past two years infiltrating Zooth's data streams and uncovering their trail of clinical fraud and reckless endangerment putting countless lives at risk."

She rooted around in the bag, producing notepads and an impressively thick dossier secured with a combination lock.

"We also have background on the key conspirators, including Zooth's CEO, Gavin Caldwell and the FDA officials they were likely bribing. Our central thesis is that Neuroloxyn was knowingly rushed to market without sufficient safety testing, resulting in over 4,000 deaths and disabilities globally over the past five years. Just for the sake of hitting an earnings window and spiking company valuation."

Thorne fixed Dr McClain with the hardest of stares, sizing up whether she truly believed what she was peddling or was just along for the ride on someone else's quixotic crusade. But her steady, unwavering eye contact and no-nonsense body language spoke to a world-weary realist unafraid of blowback or institutional retribution.

"We've built what you might call an evidentiary kill chain," she continued. "Tapping into everything from clinical study data and coroner reports to emails and memos from as high as Zooth's executive suite. All meticulously layered together to erect an ironclad, prosecutable case that fraud, malfeasance, and negligent homicides were committed on an epic scale to satisfy shareholder profit motives."

"Thrones' brow furrowed, an involuntary reaction that betrayed his subconscious intrigue. "Clearly, these three were no ordinary civilian dilettantes simply stumbling through the legal brambles based on internet claptrap. The dispassionate confidence in Dr McClain's voice and unflappable cadence spoke to genuine, procedural immersion in navigating complex professional bureaucracies.

He cleared his throat gruffly to reassert his command presence. "So, you claim to have the paper trail implicating Zooth Pharmaceuticals' execs of knowingly approving and distributing a drug they knew would harm or kill people, just to make their quarter and earn bonuses. And I suppose your next act is nominating me for sainthood too?"

Dr McClain's lips twitched subtly, fighting the urge to break composure. "We get that it seems too outrageous to be believed, even for this industry.

But our findings indicate that Neuroloxyn's' death toll might ultimately outstrip domestic cataclysms like the Opioid Crisis or Big Tobacco's lies about cancer risks. It's quite literally a 21st-century biological attack by omission that already dwarfs most terrorist events in terms of body count."

Special Agent Thorne felt his cigar stub slip from between his clenched teeth as his jaw slackened at Dr McClain's words. No hyperbole or breathless embellishment was underpinning her statement - just naked pragmatism of the highest order.

Whatever empirical construct had stiffened her academic's spine, it was enough to convince Dr McClain, and likely Dr Reynolds as well, that their proclaimed whistle-blowing struck at the absolute depravity line separating basic capitalism from crimes against humanity.

But before Thorne could formulate a response, the third unspoken member of the trio finally chimed in.

"We would have published everything already for the world to see," Amelia said in a steady, almost chillingly detached tone. "Blown the lid completely off Zooth's horrific crimes and seen them prosecuted or torn apart limb from corporation limb."

Thorne felt a frisson of electricity tingle up his spine. She definitely had his attention now.

"But then they started coming after us, trying to

shut us up by any means necessary."

With a graceful yet surprisingly unselfconscious gesture, Amelia pulled back her shoulder-length hair to reveal a sickening mass of purple and black bruising across her collarbone and neck area. It looked like someone had tried to strangle and crush her windpipe into dust.

"This is what a couple of Zooth's goons did to me in the Media House parking garage two weeks ago," she said, her China-doll features hardening into cold remineralisation. "They wanted to know what we had uncovered and to warn me off going public with anything. When strong-arming failed, they attempted to crush my larynx."

Holy Jesus, Thorne thought, feeling the blood drain from his face despite his years of working cases involving the most vicious criminals and sicko players imaginable. This was a completely different level of malice, paramilitary deterrence waged against random civilians just trying to do the right thing.

And her cautionary beating was apparently only the opening salvo in Zooth's all-out war to bury the whistleblowers intel. Dr Reynolds wordlessly pulled down his own collar to reveal the unmistakable trajectory gouges of a bullet graze along his neck.

"Two wannabe motorcycle assassins forced me off the road a few weeks before Amelia's attack," he rasped, haunted grimace etching ever deeper lines into his road-worn face. "A Single slug from a sawn-off shotgun opened me up across my neck, narrowly missing my carotid artery. Haven't slept a full night through since. You never realise just how disruptive the dreams can get after facing your own mortality in such...nihilistic terms."

Thorne felt the air turn to ice water in his lungs. These weren't just civilian crackpots rocking the boat for media celebrity or quick cash settlements. Zooth Pharmaceuticals appeared to have activated extreme deterrence protocols and fully dehumanised any potential truth-tellers to the level of enemy combatants worthy of state-sanctioned violence.

And yet here Dr Reynolds, Dr McClain, and Amelia Sinclair stood - visibly battered from the opening rounds of violence, yet still exuding steely resolve honed to tempered granite, right down to their cores. Whatever secrets they had uncovered, Zooth Pharmaceuticals' scorched-earth realpolitik had only catalysed an even greater crusading zeal for total combat.

Agent Thorne took an involuntary shuffling step backwards, appraising these whistleblowers with new eyes. He could practically feel the inferno roiling beneath their shaken exteriors, an unflagging dauntlessness to right perceived sins against humanity on a cosmic scale no matter what the personal toll. These were no mere activists or self-appointed corporate watchdogs. This was a starving lion pride united in a common cause, too woke to give up even after being violently mauled from the opening ambush.

"That's why we need to bring you in now," Dr Reynolds finally spoke again, locking eyes with the rattled FBI agent. "Before Zooth decides to permanently neutralise us with finality instead of just warning shots across the bow."

He nodded towards the overstuffed satchel in Thorne's trunk as Dr McClain thumbed the dossier's combination lock.

"Inside that kit is Pandora's locker of institutionally criminal proof tied to Neuroloxyn- backdoor FDA collusion, knowingly downplayed safety trials, illegal shadow plants pumping contraband API, you name it. This was a premeditated coverup and biological strike waged in the name of profit margins and shareholder dividends, enabled by systematic regulatory captured and shell-corporation obfuscation."

Dr Reynolds swallowed hard, purchasing Thorne's gaze with undisguised pain and primal urgency now glowing behind his eyes.

"We can no longer safeguard this intelligence, not when its very existence has put targets on our backs from faceless corporate mercenaries operating as they live above any recognisable courts or rule of law. We refuse to become the final, quieted victims of whatever slaughter Zooth has knowingly committed in the name of their damnable business model."

He gestured to the inert laptop cases and hanging-file dossiers resting in the sedan's cargo well.

"Everything is laid bare in there, surgical diagnosing of an ongoing American Medico-Homicide Event. All bundled and ready for ethical authorities to apprehend and eviscerate this hydra of depravity at the source."

Special Agent Thorne was unable to find his voice, the cords momentarily seized by the sheer magnitude of Dr Reynolds' declaration - calm and dispassionate as any surgical admission, yet lancing straight to the marrow of every social compact and civil institution is implicated as a potential unindicted co-conspirator.

Never in his career had he dreamed of touching such an electrified third rail of capitalist immorality. This went far beyond aberrations of human venality or unchecked market forces. What Dr Reynolds was alleging constituted a zero-day, existential threat to the entire epistemology and systems of authority underpinning global civilisation itself.

If their purported narrative catalogues were indeed as prophetically damning as promised....then Thorne himself might well be compromised, a dutiful son of the very same cancerously corrupted power structures Dr Reynolds and his ilk now deemed worthy of apocalyptic levels of retributive inquiry and judicial scourging.

As these refractive epiphanies ricocheted across his psyche, Special Agent Marcus Thorne felt his fingers instinctively curling around the grips of his service pistol. Not out of any urge to brandish it at these would-be whistleblowers - no, this was the trance state dread of a cornered rabbit suddenly realising the plasmic scope of its mortality and existence far transcended its mental horizons mere moments before.

Were these principled gladiators about to enlist him into a battle against the very institutions and orthodoxies he had sworn to serve, protect, and tacitly enable through undying allegiance? Or were they simply blinding manifestations of a deeper, despairing psychosis of their own creation - unmoored flagellants eager to napalm any semblance of civilisation's good-faith judicial compacts in pursuit of a scorched-earth, forced awakening of truth and accountability?

Time seemed too dilate and decelerate to a molasses crawl as Thorne stared into the gazes of each whistleblower. Dr Reynolds and his lion fangs exuded that same unyielding zeal, willing to follow the ripcord towards abyssal revelation all the way down to its nanopore roots, no matter the outcomes catalysed.

These were not mere militants or deluded radicals

ready to subvert society's unravelling tapestry with bombs or chaos as an end unto itself. No, this was the self-deputised vanguard of rigorous, evidence-driven legal and moral hawks - fronting a remorseless truth-unto-death offensive to violently purge demagogic rot from civilisations very cargo cult commissars.

And in that hyper-crystalline instant, Special Agent Thorne found his soul pierced by the unshakable realisation they were absolutely, incontrovertibly right to do so.

Even if razing every rickety convention of crooked accommodation in the process only gave rise to newer, more demented pathologies and spirals of institutionalised human indecency.

For on one side stood the unshakable proof of Law shrivelled to nothing but stripped gears and rusted wing-nuts. An infinitely bankrolled pharmaceutical Goliath feeling free to wage biological war via omission against its own tax bases and dependents. All woven into the soiled tapestry of greed and power.

And opposing it - a trio of defiant truth-tellers, wilting under black bag duress but refusing to submit to being somnambulantly silenced on behalf of their very own civilisations illusory debts and complicity.

Thorne let his scarred paw slip away from the sidearm's cosy grip, instead extending to Dr

Reynolds in open acceptance.

"I've been looking for that smoking gun against Zooth Pharmaceuticals for far too long," he growled.

CHAPTER THIRTEEN

The Unveiling

THORNE RETURNED TO his hotel room, his mind still reeling from the startling revelations that had just occurred. He carefully laid out the evidence on the bed, aware that the information before him could possibly contain the smoking gun he was searching for to unravelling the complex web of deceit and corruption. After hearing about how Zooth Pharmaceuticals had crossed the line with the trio, he understood the risks involved. There were powerful forces at play, entities willing to cross the line and go too extraordinary lengths to keep their misdeeds hidden from the public eye.

Thorne spent the better part of the night poring over the evidence, meticulously checking every detail and seeking out any inconsistencies or discrepancies. The more he read, the more his concerns grew – this was no isolated incident, but rather the culmination of a systematic effort to prioritise profits over patient welfare.

At the heart of the scandal was Zooth Pharmaceuticals, and their ground-breaking drug Neuroloxyn. The evidence before him, suggested that the company had knowingly concealed the drug's dangerous side effects, manipulated clinical trial data and bribed staff at FDA to bury the truth.

Thorne's stomach churned as he read the harrowing details of the case of Ethan Parker, the young boy whose plight had initially drawn Dr McClain to investigate the root cause behind his condition.

Zooth Pharmaceuticals had knowingly maintained

the illusion of a successful treatment, by concealing the deadly side effects of Neuroloxyn, prioritising their own financial interests over the well-being of their vulnerable patients.

As Thorne delved deeper into the files, he began to uncover a disturbing pattern of unethical practices and outright criminality. The evidence that Dr McClain and Dr Reynolds had provided him was nothing short of explosive – a trove of damning documents that painted a disturbing picture of corporate greed, medical malfeasance, and a far-reaching conspiracy that threatened to upend the entire pharmaceutical industry.

The volume and detail of the evidence that they had provided was overwhelming and Thorne spent the remainder of the night engrossed in its captivating thoroughness. It was evidently clear that Zooth Pharmaceuticals and corrupt officials at the FDA had been working in tandem.

By the time the first rays of dawn began to peek through the hotel curtains, Thorne was exhausted but resolute. He had found his smoking gun. He knew that he was sitting on a powder keg, and that the information he possessed could have far-reaching consequences.

With a renewed sense of purpose, Thorne gathered the evidence and headed to the airport, eager to get back to Miami as quickly as possible. He needed to bring his team up to speed.

The flight back to Miami was a blur, and he knew that he was about to step into a hornet's nest, and that the forces he was up against were formidable. But he was undaunted.

***

Special Agent Thorne touched down in Miami, the evidence safely secured. He was relieved to be back on familiar ground. As he exited the private jet and made his way to his car, his mind raced with the implications of what he had in his possession.

Thorne knew speed was of the essence and that he had to act quickly. Over the next month, he and his team worked tirelessly, poring over the mountain of files and carefully cross-checking every detail. He called in favours, tapped into his network of informants, and left no stone unturned.

The deeper they dug, the clearer the magnitude of the conspiracy became. They began to build their case, meticulously documenting every step of the conspiracy. Finally, after weeks of painstaking work, Thorne felt ready to bring his case to the authorities.

He arranged a meeting with the U.S. Attorney's Office, and presented his findings with the same meticulous attention to detail that had marked his entire investigation.

The prosecutors listened in stunned silence as Thorne laid out the evidence, outlining the depth and breadth of the conspiracy. They were initially sceptical, but as Thorne methodically presented the documentation, their scepticism gave way to growing alarm.

"This is... this is unbelievable," the lead prosecutor said, shaking his head. "If even a fraction of this is true, it could bring down some of the most powerful institutions in the country."

Thorne nodded grimly. "I assure you, sir, every word of it is true. And I have the evidence to prove it."

The prosecutors went into a closed meeting, weighing up the implications of moving forward with such a high-stakes case. Thorne waited patiently outside, knowing that the fate of his investigation hung in the balance.

Finally, he was called in and the lead prosecutor turned to him, a steely determination in his eyes. "Agent Thorne, you've done an outstanding job uncovering this conspiracy. We're going to take this case to a grand jury immediately. With the evidence you've provided, I believe we have a strong chance of securing indictments."

Thorne felt a surge of relief and satisfaction. After weeks of painstaking work, his efforts had paid off. But even as the prosecutors began to mobilise their resources, he couldn't shake the nagging feeling that the battle was far from over.

In the weeks that followed, the grand jury proceedings moved forward with breathtaking speed. Thorne provided detailed testimony, and the prosecutors methodically presented the mountain of evidence he had gathered. To their credit, the jurors listened with rapt attention, their faces etched with a growing sense of horror as the scope of the conspiracy became clear.

Finally, after just two weeks of deliberation, the grand jury returned a series of indictments that sent shockwaves through the medical and pharmaceutical industries.

CHAPTER FOURTEEN

The Zooth Ten

IN A SEISMIC turn of events that has rocked the pharmaceutical industry, the Executives from Zooth Pharmaceuticals, and a high-ranking official from the FDA, were simultaneously arrested by federal agents in an early morning coordinated raid. At the same time, a raid was conducted on the Miami offices of Zooth Pharmaceuticals, and had been a galactic success.

Thorne's team seized over 50 boxes of physical files and hard drives containing thousands of incriminating emails and records, before they could be destroyed. The sheer volume of the paper trail tying Zooth's highest-ranking executives to felonies was overwhelming.

Each of Zooth's top ten executive board members faced a litany of charges tying them to an alleged criminal coverup of the extreme dangers of Zooth's neurodegenerative drug Neuroloxyn.

***

Special Agent Marcus Thorne looked up from the stack of evidence files on his desk as there was a light knock on his office door. It was already ajar, and his rookie agent Dana Marris poked her head in.

"Sir, we've got the entire Zooth Pharmaceuticals executive board rounded up for interrogation," she said, unable to hide the tinge of excitement in her voice. This was the biggest case she'd been involved in since joining the FBI's healthcare fraud task force fresh out of the academy.

Thorne gave her a measured nod. "Ten individuals in total?" They had cast a wide net, determined to squeeze every last admission and scrap of evidence out of Zooth's leadership ranks.

"That's right sir," Marris confirmed. "Should I have them brought in one at a time for questioning?"

Thorne pondered the question for a moment, stroking his greying moustache pensively. He could sense Marris was eager to make her mark, to dive into the deep end and start grilling the Zooth suits immediately. But he knew a more methodical approach was required, especially when it came to the sculpted legal manoeuvring they'd undoubtedly attempt.

"Not yet," he said finally. "Let's get them processed and separated first. Put them in isolated holding rooms, make sure there's no way for them to get their stories straight before we start interrogations."

" I want you, in the meantime, to get full dossiers on every one of those Zooth pricks so we know exactly what kinds of snakes we're dealing with."

Marris nodded and swiftly collected the data from the forensic analysts who had been combing through Zooth's server backups and archives. In under an hour, she had compiled detailed background profiles on Gavin Caldwell, Zooth's CEO, as well as the nine other executives.

Caldwell was the kingpin, the diabolical mastermind orchestrating Zooth's illicit practices from the top. A 56-year-old Wharton finance grad, he had come up through the ranks of Big Pharma. An arrogant narcissist accustomed to doing whatever it took to get ahead, Caldwell had desperately tried covering up the fact that Neuroloxyn was killing patients. His motive was simple — keeping the catastrophically flawed drug on the market and reaping its massive profits at any cost.

As for the nine-member Zooth board who had facilitated and signed off on Caldwell's misdeeds, their names and backgrounds were as follows:

- Dante Underhill, 60, Chief Financial Officer – A silver-haired number-cruncher straight out of central casting, Underhill had been at Zooth Pharmaceuticals for over 15 years. He oversaw the fraudulent accounting practices used to hide the tremendous overhead Neuroloxyn's disastrous side effects caused the company.

- Rajesh Patel, 49, Chief Medical Officer – Born in Mumbai, Patel received his medical degree from Stanford before rising through Big Pharma's ranks to become Zooth Pharmaceutical's top scientist. He personally oversaw the falsification of Neuroloxyn's clinical safety data and lied to the FDA on multiple occasions when questioned about its side effects.

- Griffin Kesser, 46, VP Regulatory Affairs –

A weaselly career corporate lawyer, Kesser was in charge of all regulatory matters. He crafted the internal strategy to strategically bribe FDA officials and get Zooth Pharmaceuticals dangerous new products rubber-stamped for market.

- Nova Hollingsworth, 38, VP Marketing – A cold, ambitious woman who would do anything to ascend Zooth Pharmaceuticals corporate ladder, Hollingsworth spearheaded the fraudulent marketing tactics claiming Neuroloxyn was safer and less addictive than other similar drugs on the market.

- Atlas Jenner, 53, VP Manufacturing – Overseeing Zooth Pharmaceuticals production pipeline, Jenner ignored safety protocols and quality control standards to push more Neuroloxyn out the door at lower costs, exacerbating the drug's dangers.

- Wallace Tanaka, 62, VP East Asia Operations – Tanaka facilitated shadow factories in China used to manufacture Neuroloxyn's ingredients and active compounds in unregulated facilities with zero oversight.

- Haruki Aso, 48, VP West Asia Operations – Tanaka's counterpart for Zooth Pharmaceuticals' Indian operations, Also oversaw the same shady offshoring practices to keep Neuroloxyn's production pipeline humming along unimpeded.

- Heinrich Gerken, 51, VP European Operations – The head of Zooth Pharmaceuticals business across the Atlantic, Gerken denied the medical establishment's concerns over Neuroloxyn's dangers and aggressively expanded sales efforts around the continent.

- Lyra Velazquez, 43, Chief Legal Officer – Zooth Pharmaceuticals lead counsel who oversaw the mass shredding of documentation and emails related to Neuroloxyn's deadly side effects. She also attempted multiple cover-ups and stonewalled all federal investigations.

Agent Thorne read through each profile carefully, committing every lurid detail to memory. The rot of greed and deception had reached into every facet of Zooth's global operations and corporate hierarchy. It was a cancerous growth that clearly needed to be burned out with radical surgery.

"Marris, did our tech team manage to decrypt those emails from Caldwell's private servers?" Thorne asked, putting the profiles down on his desk.

"Yes sir, still working on it but they've pulled a few dozen so far. I'll get you the highlights."

Twenty minutes later, Marris returned with a newly printed dossier. "You'll want to see these," she said grimly.

Thorne flipped through the document, his face darkening with every page. The emails painted a clear picture of Caldwell and his C-suite actively conspiring to deceive government regulators, silence whistleblowers, and double down on peddling Neuroloxyn in wilful disregard for the lives being lost.

Crass messages were joking about Neuroloxyn's body count, vicious threats to any employees who considered going to authorities, and meticulous instructions on keeping two separate books to hide the drug's true risks and costs from shareholders.

Finally, Thorne came across a brash message from just six weeks ago, sent from Caldwell's personal address to the entire Zooth executive board.

It read:

"Gentlemen and ladies, it's become abundantly clear that the government's witch hunt against our company is intensifying. They've been sniffing around Neuroloxyn's safety data for months, no doubt prompted by all the meritless lawsuits from those shysters.

Well, I say no more. We're going to strangle this snake in its crib, quickly and quietly. Our friends at the FDA have agreed to make this all go away with a few million strategically donated dollars to their re-election campaigns. As for Neuroloxyn's manufacturing, we're shifting all active ingredient production to our special facilities in mainland China. Those Triad-backed contractors certainly know how to cover their tracks when any nosy inspectors come sniffing around.

Enclosed are the new handbook addendums with details for switching all sensitive data and communications over to encrypted channels. Plausible deniability will be our best friend over the next few months. No more paperwork trails, no more smoking guns for the feds to get cute with.

Let's make this problem go away quickly and get back to printing money, people.

Our shareholders are counting on us.

Warm regards,

Gavin

Thorne had seen enough. He closed the dossier, his face tightening with righteous indignation. This was so much bigger than just another corporate scandal — this was malicious, premeditated murder for hire on a massive scale in the name of profit. And all orchestrated by some of the wealthiest, most powerful people in the country.

He stood up forcefully, knocking his chair backwards with a clatter. "Get those Zooth scumbags in here right now," Thorne growled at

Agent Marris. "I want them all sweating in separate interrogation rooms until they start spilling their guts."

He snatched the file up and stomped out of his office towards the interrogation rooms. "We're taking these bastards straight to RICO court if it's the last thing I do."

Thorne, Marris, and a team of federal prosecutors interrogated the Zooth Ten, as the case was nicknamed. Without the protective shield of their corporate empire's litigation machine, the illusion of executive privilege and untouchability quickly crumbled. Their smug bravado facade vanished as agents presented damning evidence directly tying the individuals to outright felonies.

One by one, and upon the advice of their lawyers, seven lower-level executives began to fold under the onslaught of evidence against them. In exchange for cooperating with prosecutors, the seven were permitted to turn state's evidence against Gavin Caldwell, Dante Underhill, and Lyra Velazquez in exchange for a reduced sentence.

Even when confronted with the overwhelming mass of evidence against him, Caldwell, with his arrogant narcissism, sneered at the mere notion that he could ever face consequences. He believed himself to be untouchable. Following an intensive interrogation session, he still feebly attempted to assert plausibility and refute the deadly effects of Neuroloxyn. His narcissistic personality prevented him from taking any accountability, even when agents confronted the CEO with internal memos proving he had been aware of the lethal side effects from the beginning and had pushed for the drug's release anyway to meet aggressive sales projections.

Dante Underhill and Lyra Velazquez both lawyered up and refused to talk.

The three heaviest hitters, Gavin Caldwell, Dante Underhill, and Lyra Velazquez, faced over two dozen charges each under the Racketeer Influenced and Corrupt Organisations Act (RICO), a potent federal law designed to dismantle crime families and massive fraud operations.

Their offences included racketeering, money laundering, bribery, safety violations, attempted murder and most severely — second-degree murder for the thousands of patient deaths caused by their corporate malfeasance. If convicted at trial, all three would likely face multiple life sentences with no chance of parole.

The RICO case against Zooth Pharmaceuticals became a seminal event for the Department of Justice cracking down on corporate criminal behaviour in the healthcare sector. Over 40 different federal agencies assisted in building the case using novel prosecutorial tactics to finally hold the drug giant's executive leadership directly accountable for its misdeeds.

Scores of pill mill operators, pharmacists, street

dealers, and even doctors had previously been convicted for illegal opioid distribution causing fatal overdoses and tied to the ongoing epidemic. But the Feds had yet to set a precedent for treating corporate pharmaceutical manufacturers as murderous entities when their flagship products proved dangerous and killed consumers. That could all change with the Zooth Pharmaceuticals prosecution.

As the indictments were unsealed and the accused were arraigned, it became clear that the defendants had access to some of the most powerful legal minds in the country. They mounted a fierce and well-resourced defence, employing every tactic in the book to delay the proceedings and sow doubt in the minds of the public.

***

At a press conference U.S. Attorney Jessica Wheeler announced the indictments.

"I can confirm that early this morning ten executive board members from Zooth Pharmaceuticals and a high-ranking official from the FDA were simultaneously arrested by federal agents in coordinated raids. Three former top executives have been indicted by a federal grand jury. The 124-count indictment includes startling allegations that the executives recklessly and knowingly oversaw the marketing and sale of a drug called Neuroloxyn, despite being aware of its severe side effects," announced Jessica Wheeler.

"As this is an ongoing investigation I cannot comment further."

The news media seized on the story, devoting wall-to-wall coverage to the unfolding scandal. Thorne watched with a mixture of satisfaction and trepidation as the story unfolded, knowing that the real battle was only just beginning.

CHAPTER FIFTEEN

Court

THE LONG-AWAITED trial date arrived, and the tension in the courtroom was palpable. Caldwell, Underhill, and Velazquez had spared no expense in their defence, assembling a formidable team of lawyers and expert witnesses. They were determined to overwhelm the prosecution with a flood of technical jargon and obfuscation.

But Thorne and the prosecutors were equally determined. They had spent months meticulously preparing their case, and they were confident in the strength of the evidence. As the trial began, they methodically laid out the story of the conspiracy, calling a parade of witnesses and introducing a seemingly endless stream of documents and exhibits.

The defence fought back with every tool in their arsenal, objecting to the admission of evidence, challenging the credibility of witnesses, and launching relentless attacks on the prosecution's case. But Jessica Wheeler and her team refused to be rattled, calmly and confidently countering each move with a meticulous rebuttal.

The trial dragged on for weeks, and the public's attention began to waver. The defendants and their allies launched a concerted media blitz, portraying themselves as the victims of a witch hunt and casting doubt on the integrity of the proceedings.

But the prosecution remained undeterred. They knew that the truth was on their side, and they were determined to see justice served. Ms Wheeler spent long hours poring over the evidence, searching for any inconsistency or weakness that the defence might try to exploit.

Finally, after weeks of gruelling testimony and fierce legal wrangling, the case was submitted to the jury. Thorne and his team waited with bated breath as the jurors deliberated, knowing that the fate of the entire investigation hung in the balance.

After three agonising days, the jury returned with their verdict.

From the gallery seating just a few rows up, Thorne could see the three defendants - Gavin Caldwell, Dante Underhill, and Lyra Velazquez - trying futilely to maintain their composure as the jury filed in.

***

Caldwell was already starting to sweat through his pressed shirt, his bravado from earlier clearly shaken. Next to him, Underhill was biting his lip anxiously, the hollow bags under his eyes indicating many sleepless nights spent agonising over his impending legal fate.

Only Velazquez maintained her trademark icy demeanour, staring straight ahead impassively as judge Raymond Torres entered and called the court to order. But even she couldn't completely mask the slight snarl that crinkled her upper lip — a subtle hint at the growing apprehension she felt.

"Members of the jury," demanded Judge Torres in a stern tone, wasting no time on preamble. "have you reached a verdict?"

The foreman, a bookish man in his early forties, stood up stiffly as if preparing to deliver a grand oration. "We have, your honour."

Thorne felt a knot of anticipation tightening in his gut. After dedicating years of his life to pursuing this case, the stakes could not possibly be higher. A conviction on the major charges would set a historic legal precedent and send shockwaves through every pharmaceutical boardroom that executives could finally be held criminally culpable for peddling fatally unsafe products solely in pursuit of profits.

Conversely, an acquittal would render the entire operation futile — a toothless slap that would signal a failed effort, even after thousands of deaths, these corporate kingpins could continue their illicit practices unencumbered, hidden behind limited liability laws and armies of high-priced lawyers. It would be a devastating defeat.

"On the charges of federal racketeering, fraud, conspiracy, and money laundering..." how do you find Gavin Caldwell?" Asked Judge Torres.

The ambiance within the courthouse was palpably heavy, as if one could cut through it with a knife.

"On the charges of federal racketeering, fraud, conspiracy, and money laundering..." the foreman began slowly, building tense drama, "this jury finds Gavin Caldwell,... guilty on all counts."

"On the charges of federal racketeering, conspiracy, and money laundering..." how do you find Dante Underhill?"

"This jury finds Dante Underhill...guilty on all counts."

"On the charges of federal racketeering, fraud, conspiracy, and money laundering..." how do you find Lyra Velazquez?"

"This jury finds Lyra Velazquez...guilty on all counts."

A murmur swept across the courtroom, but Thorne remained stone-faced and stoic, his arms folded tightly. That was simply setting the table — par for the course in a white-collar case this large. Now came the main course that would determine whether this prosecution truly made history or fizzled into irrelevance.

The foreman shuffled his papers and cleared his throat loudly.

"On the charges of second-degree murder under the Racketeer Influenced and Corrupt Organisations Act..." how do you find Gavin Caldwell?" asked judge Torres.

"On the charges of second-degree murder under the Racketeer Influenced and Corrupt Organisations

Act..." the foreman began, "this jury finds Gavin Caldwell … guilty."

"On the charges of second-degree murder under the Racketeer Influenced and Corrupt Organisations Act..." how do you find Dante Underhill?"

"...this jury finds Dante Underhill … guilty."

"On the charges of second-degree murder under the Racketeer Influenced and Corrupt Organisations Act..." how do you find Lyra Velazquez?"

"...this jury finds Lyra Velazquez … guilty."

The words hung in the air like a shockwave, outright gasps and cheering erupted from the stunned spectators. For the first time in American corporate history, pharmaceutical executives now officially stood convicted of murder — just like street thugs or drug cartel kingpins peddling lethal narcotics. The message was as clear as the dumbstruck, disbelieving look on the faces of the three Zooth ringleaders.

Thorne felt a profound sense of achievement and catharsis sweeping over him. Finally, the legal loophole permitting so much corporate homicide and criminality to go unaddressed had been closed. No longer could these wolves simply settle lawsuits or pay relatively paltry fines, then walk away scot-free when their deceit and cutting corners resulted in death on a mass scale.

The very real threat of hard prison time for the

capitalist elite had arrived. And with it, a monumental power shift reverberating throughout entire industries and corridors of capitalism itself.

"The sentencing hearing will reconvene in two days." Instructed judge Raymond Torres

Gavelling the courtroom into recess , Caldwell, Underhill and Velazquez were lead away to lockup.

Families of victims swarmed forward to tearfully shake Thorne's hand, the gruff FBI agent simply let out a long sigh and cracked a rare smile of grim satisfaction.

"Well, I'll be damned," he muttered quietly, still trying to process the enormity of the jury's verdict. "Sometimes the good guys really do win one for the history books."

***

The scene outside the federal courthouse was a raucous madhouse as the verdict reached the public. Throngs of reporters and camera crews had gathered, eagerly awaiting the prosecution team to emerge and make their statement.

When U.S. Attorney Jessica Wheeler finally appeared, she had to shove her way through a scrum of microphones and lights being shoved in her face by the frenzied press corps. Every major national outlet was jostling for position to get her reaction to the historic rulings.

Wheeler held up her hands to temporarily calm the melee. She could see the ravenous pack of journalists was practically foaming at the mouth after witnessing the precedent-shattering murder convictions against Zooth Pharma's criminal leadership.

"Ladies and gentlemen, please!" Wheeler shouted over the cacophony. "Justice has been served, I'll take a few questions, but let's have some order."

She pointed at a grizzled veteran reporter from the New York Times. "You first."

"U.S. Attorney Wheeler, these convictions on second-degree murder charges are unprecedented for pharmaceutical executives," the reporter bellowed. "What kind of message do you hope this sends to the industry?"

Wheeler paused for a beat to allow the understatement to hang in the air. Finally, she responded with steely gravitas.

"Let me be unambiguous — this verdict represents a seismic shift and lays down a blazing bright line in the sand," she stated firmly. "For decades, big pharmaceutical companies have turned a blind eye to patient safety, prioritising earnings and profits over human lives. They've been able to write off criminal penalties and fines as simply the cost of doing business."

She shook her head with disgust. "Well, those days are over. If you intentionally peddle an unsafe drug that kills or injures people in the ruthless pursuit of making more money, you can now be held criminally culpable just like a street dealer pushing lethal narcotics."

Wheeler's words sent a hush over the crowd, letting the weight of her message sink in. She was not mincing words — this was a direct threat to every pharmaceutical C-suite and boardroom in America.

"No more hiding behind limited liability laws or insulating top brass through a corporate veil," Wheeler continued, her voice rising with intensity. "If you are convicted of racketeering leading to loss of life, you're going to face hard prison time just like any other murderer. End of story."

The reporters instantly began shouting new questions, recognising they were witnessing a pivotal moment that would reverberate for generations in the industry. Wheeler motioned for quiet again.

"I have been prosecuting pharmaceutical cases and corporate crimes for over 20 years," she stated with a hint of weariness. "I have grown tired of seeing a justice system that applies one set of rules to the wealthy and well-connected, while the rest of society is held to another. That changes today with this verdict."

She stared down the camera lenses with a fiery certitude. "To the entire global pharmaceutical industry, I say this — proactively get your houses in order and take a long hard look at reforming your systemic practices. Because a conviction like this one shows we will not hesitate to bring the full force of the law upon anyone prioritising profit over safety and human life."

With that parting salvo, Wheeler turned and strode away through the scrum, leaving the press gaggle awestruck and energised to spread word of the momentous ruling to every corner of the commercial world. A new era of corporate accountability had dawned — the free pass was officially over.

CHAPTER SIXTEEN
Sentencing

TWO DAYS LATER, the courthouse was again swarming with reporters and camera crews as the sentencing phase for the Zooth Pharmaceuticals executives convicted of racketeering, fraud, conspiracy, money laundering, and the historic second-degree murder charges was set to begin.

Inside the tense courtroom, the gallery seating was packed to capacity with victims' families, advocates, and media hoping to witness the life sentences that prosecutors had made clear they would be pursuing.

When U.S. District Judge Raymond Torres took the bench, a hush fell over the proceedings. He surveyed the room sternly before addressing the three convicted defendants - Gavin Caldwell, Dante Underhill, and Lyra Velazquez.

"I trust you all understand the extent of your crimes and the reasons we are here today," the judge intoned gravely. "You have been found guilty by a jury of your peers of racketeering, fraud, money laundering, and most critically — second-degree murder under the RICO statutes for your roles in conspiring to conceal the extreme dangers posed by your company's drug Neuroloxyn."

Torres paused to let the weight of the latter charge resonate. It was the first time in American legal history that pharmaceutical executives had been convicted of actual murder charges for prioritising profits over public safety.

"Your actions — systematically hiding evidence

and lying about the side effects that cost over 4,000 patient lives — represent a shocking criminal breach of trust," the judge continued, his voice laced with disgust. "You have been entrusted as leaders of a pharmaceutical firm with an ethical and moral obligation to ensure your products are genuinely safe and effective for public use. Instead, you chose to deceive, obfuscate, and cover up the truth that people were dying."

Torres's withering gaze swept over the three defendants who remained stone-faced and betrayed no emotion. He scowled with contempt.

"Not only that, but you took reprehensible steps to violently intimidate and kill whistleblowers and truth-tellers within your own company who tried to shed light on these unconscionable practices. The jury has definitively exposed your corporation as a criminal enterprise that wilfully and intentionally cost human lives in your pursuit of revenue."

A heavy silence hung in the air, pierced only by occasional stifled sobs from grieving family members. Torres cleared his throat to press on with the sentencing.

"In light of their involvement in these incomprehensible transgressions, the United States government is formally petitioning for Mr Caldwell, Mr Underhill, and Ms Velazquez to be sentenced to life imprisonment without the chance of parole." A smattering of gasps and cries erupted from the gallery before the Torres silenced them by rapping his gavel.

"I have reviewed the evidence, victim statements, and sentencing recommendations extensively," Torres stated grimly. "And although I find the government's requested term of life in prison to be absolutely warranted given the sheer magnitude of corporate criminality, greed, and loss of human life involved."

He turned his gaze directly to the three defendants seated impassively at the defendant's table.

"You are now convicted felons, guilty of murder and racketeering. You effectively operated an illegal drug cartel peddling fatal products while brushing aside the bodies through corruption and cover-ups. You abused positions of prime societal trust for personal enrichment without an ounce of regard for public well-being."

Torres's voice rose with righteous fury. "Let this verdict send a resounding message that such conduct will no longer be tolerated or minimised through meagre fines and lapdog settlements. If you are a pharmaceutical executive who wilfully causes death through corporate malfeasance, you will be viewed no differently than a street felon slaying innocents."

A tense hush blanketed the courtroom as Torres composed himself briefly.

After allowing Caldwell, Underhill and Velazquez one final chance to make statements and plead for leniency, he began delivering his rulings.

"Mr Caldwell, this court has taken into account the shocking patterns of racketeering, money laundering, fraud, bribery, and murder in the second degree which were thoroughly proven at trial. As the ringleader of these unconscionable criminal acts which continued in the face of mounting patient deaths tied to Zooth's product, Neuroloxyn, I sentence you to life in federal prison, without the possibility of parole..."

The words hit Caldwell like a ton of bricks, his head slumping as he mouthed silent words of disbelief. He'd arrogantly deemed himself lord of his Pharma empire, untouchable and insulated behind the legal bureaucracies. Now that facade had been obliterated.

Underhill's turn came next. "Mr Underhill, in light of your position as chief financial officer and your involvement in racketeering, money laundering, fraud, and bribery, which resulted in the loss of lives due to your company's gross negligence, this court hereby imposes a sentence of 25 years' imprisonment upon you, without the possibility of parole..."

The former executive's wife let out a muffled wail, burying her face in her hands as the gravity of his sentence cemented. For once, the cocky number-cruncher was reduced to silence, his eyes staring vacantly as visions of his twilight years being stripped away game crashing around him.

Finally, Torres turned his tongue-lashing towards Velazquez. "Ms Velazquez, as a member of the bar who swore an oath to uphold the law, your calculated decisions to flagrantly obstruct investigations and statutes through bribes, falsehoods and threats represent a devastating breach of public trust. For your role in this expansive criminal conspiracy, this court sentences you to 25 years behind bars, without the possibility of parole..."

Velazquez remained stoic, her flinty veneer never cracking despite the de facto life sentence being handed down. Even striped of her freedom until geriatric, she steadfastly refused to show any hint of the remorse or accountability she'd eschewed throughout.

The courthouse had descended into chaos after Judge Raymond Torres read out the punishingly lengthy prison sentences for Zooth Pharmaceuticals' felonious leadership trio.

Protesters and victims' families openly wept, cheered, and embraced, emotionally overloaded by the prospect of Caldwell, Underhill and Velazquez being ripped from their lavish lifestyles and entombed behind bars for decades as a reckoning for their crimes.

But Torres wasn't done twisting the screws on the corporate criminals just yet.

After a brief recess to let the feverish atmosphere cool slightly, he recalled the court to order and trained his sights squarely on Lyra Velazquez.

As Zooth's former chief legal officer, she had ostensibly once sworn a solemn oath to uphold the rule of law as a member of the bar. But as the jury determined, Velazquez had become a font of corruption herself — strategically undermining those very laws through bribery, intimidation, lies and obstructing the pursuit of justice at every turn.

All of it was in service of shielding the truth about Neuroloxyn's catastrophic human toll from regulators, prescribers and the public while protecting the illegal windfall profits. Her unethical actions formed the crux of the racketeering conspiracy by Zooth's criminal leadership.

"Ms Velazquez, please stand to be addressed further," Torres stern voice echoed through the hushed courtroom.

Slowly, Velazquez rose to her feet, back ramrod straight, eyes forward in a defiant stare. Even after the guilty verdicts, after being condemned to spending her senior years behind bars instead of on a lavish retirement, the disgraced attorney remained stubbornly imperious.

Torres levelled his gaze at her unmoved countenance before speaking again, his tone carrying hints of disgusted contempt.

"You have displayed a shocking disregard and enmity for the legal profession's ethical standards to which you swore a sworn duty," he said firmly. "An oath I assume you took with all intended solemnity when first admitted to the bar as an officer of the court."

Torres paused, seemingly searching Velazquez's face for any flicker of remorse or comprehension of the systemic abuses of trust she'd enabled. Finding none, he pressed on inexorably.

"Your criminal actions represent a fundamental assault on the public's faith in our judicial system and the honourable vocation of jurisprudence itself," Torres declared with escalating gravity. "Conduct so repugnant and antithetical, it quite simply cannot be tolerated from one entrusted as a gatekeeper of ethical legal practice."

Velazquez remained unblinkingly stoic, even as Torres words landed like a cold slap of harsh reality cutting through the forced indifference.

"Therefore, in addition to your prison sentence, I am compelled to completely disbar you from ever again practicing law before any court in this nation," Torres stated with finality. "You are officially stripped of the privilege to stand as an advocate for pursuing justice and truth."

The words hung in the air like a searing brand, a complete professional immolation for the once high-powered corporate counsel. As the reality sank in, Velazquez imperceptibly blinked hard once, the first crack in her statuesque facade during the entire process.

"Take her into custody," Torres ordered flatly.

As federal marshals quickly moved to re-shackle her, Velazquez's eyes flashed briefly with a hint of the unadulterated rage and entitlement that had powered her criminal decision-making. A silent fury at having everything stripped away that she'd spent her life accruing through graft and moral vacancy.

But it was too little, far too late. No more shady backroom leveraging or parlour tricks by a defrocked lawyer who'd gambled everything on a pack of lies — and lost it all.

As the sentencing continued to descend on Zooth's cadre of underlings and collaborator, Judge Torres made one thing resoundingly clear. The legal ramifications for this criminal big Pharma enterprise would span decades and redefine how corporate obsolesce and avarice enabling mass fatalities was adjudicated from now on.

***

Outside, the verdicts set off raucous cheers and applause from protesters and advocates who had worked tirelessly to see this judicial reckoning achieved. One by one, they pumped their fists and chanted the now-iconic words that would become a rallying cry symbolising this landmark case:

"PILL THEM UNDER THE JAIL!"

CHAPTER SEVENTEEN

The Suicide Manifest

AS THE GUARDS drew near, the resonance of their approaching steps shattered the eerie silence. One of them reached down and felt for a pulse, shaking his head grimly he confirmed what they'd already suspected. The mighty Caldwell, the philandering pharmaceutical kingpin who had so brazenly defied authorities through bribery and intimidation, was no more.

The eerie stillness that permeated the cellblock was suffocating. Gavin Caldwell's body lay motionless on the cold, unforgiving floor of his 8x10 concrete tomb, face frozen in a lifeless grimace. His once vibrant eyes, which had radiated arrogance and steely determination, were now dull and vacant orbs devoid of the swagger that had propelled him to dizzying heights of power.

The guards remained silent, their stoic presence contrasting sharply with the bedsheet wound tightly around his neck, a grim testament to his demise. Once a towering figure of power, his empire, constructed through deceit and ruthlessness, now loomed over him as a haunting spectre within these prison walls. It served as a bitter reminder of the arrogance that led to his spectacular collapse. In a final act of desperation, the man who had once played recklessly with the lives of many had now wagered the only life he had left—his own.

In the stifling silence, the faint drip of water from a leaky pipe was the only sound that could be heard, a hollow, echoing rhythm that seemed to taunt Caldwell's diminished state.

Within hours, the news reverberated like a thunderclap — first through the dank prison corridors, then rippling outward until it consumed the nation's ravenous appetite for updates on the fallen titan's fate. Gavin Caldwell, 57 years old and just three weeks into a life sentence, was dead by his own hand.

For the families of Neuroloxyn's victims, it was a truth that offered no sense of closure or catharsis — only compounded outrage that this remorseless charlatan had cheated true accountability through the ultimate act of cowardice. They had deserved to see him suffer, to wither behind bars as penance for the thousands of agonising deaths he'd so wilfully enabled.

Yet for others, particularly those still picking up the pieces of public trust badly shattered, Caldwell's demise prompted more curiosity than contempt.

Had the once swaggering CEO finally encountered a reckoning too vast to rationalise away with his labyrinthine delusions? What deep, dark secrets about his crimes did he take to the grave — final truths untold that could facilitate more meaningful justice or systemic reforms to inoculate society from such corporate butchers moving forward?

Or was this simply the pathetic final salvo of someone so irredeemably empty inside that even during society's hour recompense, his sole priority remained unconditional self-preservation through whatever means remained?

As armchair analysts, pundits and columnists endlessly dissected the tragedy from their computer-lit bubbles, the grim reality within those dreary prison walls told a more visceral tale. One of what scarce few personal belongings remained in Caldwell's spartan cell in the aftermath — a rambling, 27-page handwritten manifesto delivered like a dead man's last selfish gasps to steal back his narrative from the jaws of ignominy.

Its slashing, vitriolic screeds cursed those who had endeavoured to bring down his criminal empire, casting their crusade against him as "a soulless had of profiteers and moral quarries enabled by ignorant media lapdogs." Yet his words also betrayed tell-tale signs of raw delusion and self-mythologizing, rife with persecution complexities and fabrications intended to reframe his crimes as mere "proactive triage safeguarding innovation's vanguard."

In essence, the bitter jeremiad was a final, pathetic attempt by a desperate inmate to rewrite the immutable truth of his toxic wake - a counterfactual where society had simply failed to recognise his warped vision of societal betterment through unfettered profiteering.

But beneath the bluster and self-gaslighting, perceptive interpreters glimpsed flashes of something else - a haunting spectre of regret weighed down by guilt's burden, too heavy for even his mercenary hubris to deflect forever. Snippets where the real Gavin Caldwell resurfaced like a cornered rat through the hairline cracks of his narcissistic armour, his words betraying flashes of remorse, self-loathing and anguish gnawing away at his conscience.

"I let the means become the end," he scribbled at one point, his handwriting devolving into a scrawl as if euphemisms alone could no longer mask the truth. "Always convincing myself that the millions of lives I was trading were justified by the macro vision...distilled casualties for humanity's greater good amidst the clinical dialectic of market plagues naturally culling society."

Yet, these islands of clarity and penance would re-emerge only fleetingly in a sea of tirades projecting blame and rationalising his misdeeds through opiating corporate jargon. Whatever revelatory wellspring of Caldwell's own private self-awareness existed, he never chiselled down through its detached, clinical calcification to find the core of feeling and accountable manhood.

Inevitably, his fragmented, meandering manuscript concluded with as much certainty as the life animating its feverish scratching had.

"I am the tip of an arrow already loosed, fired from the benign apathy and amorality coursing through capitalism's great human centipede. I alone stand convicted, but I am not alone."

With that bitter epitaph and self-cast martyrdom, the voice trailed off into smeared ink blots and insensible scribbling. Gavin Caldwell, unrepentant charlatan, and condemned soul to his final breaths, had played his final hand - presenting a literary corpse every bit as devoid of meaningful depth or substance as the human who birthed it.

Some speculated that he had been silenced to prevent him from revealing incriminating information about other high-profile figures. Others believed that guilt and shame had finally caught up with him, driving him to take his own life rather than face the consequences of his actions.

But regardless of the circumstances, Caldwell's death marked the end of an era. The reign of terror that had gripped Zooth Pharmaceuticals was over, but the scars it left behind would take years to heal.

Only the compressed tang of chemical entropy filling his cell offered true finality and silence at long last.

CHAPTER EIGHTEEN

A Regulator's Reckoning

THE ZOOTH PHARMACEUTICALS scandal reached even further tendrils of disgrace as the final dominos toppled in courtroom dramatics months later. On a crisp autumn morning, the nation turned its attention to federal district court in Boston, where another act in the sordid crime story was playing out.

Richard Barkly, a former senior official in the FDA Office of New Drugs, stood ramrod straight before the judge's bench. His jaw was clenched tightly, but the aged bureaucrat's eyes remained downcast as he awaited sentencing for his central role enabling Zooth's litany of criminal acts.

The evidence presented at Barkly's trial proved not just a dereliction of regulatory duty in overlooking Neuroloxyn's shoddy data and risk signals. No, this was a cold-blooded and premeditated conspiracy of collusion with Zooth's leadership.

Email and financial records entered into evidence showed Barkly had been on the take for over a decade—receiving millions in kickbacks from Zooth funnelled through an offshore banking laundromat. In exchange, he ran interference on FDA oversight activities and approvals, his involvement extended beyond Neuroloxyn, burying negative data about drugs under threat of audit findings against the company.

Even more damningly, witnesses testified about Barkly's direct role in actively suppressing complaints from his own FDA colleagues as they tried raising red flags about the drug's safety profile. More than once, he threatened reprisals and terminations against those going outside his chain of command.

In essence, Barkly had effectively functioned as a corporate mole within the government's regulatory apparatus—selling out his constitutional duties time and again to line his pockets at the behest of Zooth.

"This offence represents a shattering fall from grace virtually unrivalled within the federal workforce," Judge Aliya Chaudry stated in an icy tone as she prepared to render Barkly's sentence. "One which cuts to the very heart of our ethical obligations to safeguard public health at all costs."

The judge paused for a beat, pivoting her gaze to lock squarely on the disgraced official as if attempting to bore lasers into his bowed posture.

"Through greed, cowardice and lack of even fundamental morality, you enabled corporate actors to quite literally get away with murder and mass bodily harm for a price," she continued with smouldering indignation. "Thereby betraying every citizen trusting your solemn charge as a watchdog over the guardians keeping us safe from harm."

Barkly remained utterly motionless and impassive as Chaudry's censure washed over him like an inquisitor's lash. Only the faintest muscle tic in his jaw hinted at an internalised anguish over the crushing legacy of his own treachery.

"For these reasons," the judge pressed on firmly, "and despite your formerly unblemished record in public service, I am compelled to impose the fullest possible sentence in hopes it serves clear deterrence for any other bad actors debasing the public trust through wanton avarice."

With that, Chaudry straightened the crisp judicial robe over her slender frame and delivered the final pronouncement.

"Richard Barkly, this court hereby sentences you to 25 years' imprisonment in a federal corrections facility. You are to serve every day of that term without possibility of parole..."

An audible gasp echoed through the courtroom gallery. Even among the most jaded observers, a sentence of quarter-century immurement for a senior regulatory official was nothing short of breathtaking in its severity.

But Chaudry was resolute in underscoring the gravity of Barkly's crimes, hammering her gavel forcefully as court officers moved in. Shackles were quickly affixed to the old man's wrists and ankles as the realisation sank in that he'd effectively been condemned to die behind bars.

Yet even engulfed in these grim circumstances, Barkly remained devoid of palpable remorse or pleas for mercy as he was led away to fold into the federal prison system. The soul-deadened visage of a mercenary utterly calloused to the wake of his profiteering misdeeds.

In the aftermath, however, the searing imagery of this once-esteemed public servant being marched off in chains sent shockwaves reverberating throughout the federal workforce and permanently calcified public perceptions.

How could foundational institutions sworn to protect citizens from harm so thoroughly fail on such a systemic scale? What deeper institutional toxins still metastasised uncured that enabled the collusive rot at FDA's core?

While Zooth's corporate titans already stood convicted and disgraced for their entrepreneurial savagery, the subsequent Barkly affair only inflamed undercurrents of seething mistrust towards those regulating society's fragile guard rails.

In other words, the message was chillingly clear — not even the so-called good apples among Washington's regulatory machine were automatically worthy of blanket public faith anymore. And the restorative road ahead to rebuilding that vital trust would undoubtedly prove long, winding and serpentine.

CHAPTER NINETEEN

Watchdog Turned Accomplice

IN THE SEISMIC wake of the Zooth Pharmaceuticals convictions, reverberations immediately began rippling outward across the entire pharmaceutical industry ecosystem. It was apparent the systemic failures enabling such egregious corporate criminality went far deeper than a single rogue company.

At the eye of the storm was the FDA - the very regulatory agency tasked with safeguarding public health and safety. How could a pharmaceutical product as lethally flawed as Neuroloxyn have so comprehensively evaded oversight during Zooth's manipulations and cover-up?

The question haunted FDA Commissioner Laura Rifkin as she absorbed the withering reproach in the aftermath of the shocking convictions. It soon became clear that rungs within her own bureaucracy were undoubtedly compromised, crippled by institutional inertia, underfunding, revolving door cosiness with industry — or potentially even deeper-rooted graft and malfeasance.

Rifkin knew the agency's reputation was haemorrhaging credibility at a potentially existential rate. Drastic measures were required to attempt restoring even a semblance of public trust before it corroded completely.

Within days, the FDA commissioner formally announced the creation of the Bioren Special Investigative Branch - an internal purge empowered to root out corruption, collusion, and negligence by any means necessary. At its helm, Rifkin installed Patricia Bioren, a former U.S. Attorney renowned for her implacable prosecutorial zeal.

"This investigation will be thorough, it will be unsparing, and it will reshape FDA's culture from the ground up if required," Rifkin stated grimly at their introductory press conference. "Anyone obstructing or impeding this process will be immediately terminated and subject to potential criminal referral."

Bioren herself took the podium next, green eyes flashing with determination as she sized up the camera's intense scrutiny.

"Let me be blunt — this agency has suffered a catastrophic breach of its core mission," she stated with a steely Texas drawl. "The public's faith and Zooth's victims demand an accounting and reckoning for how such unconscionable regulatory failures were allowed to enable mass fatalities and criminality at every level."

She paused, jaw clenching subtly as the gravity of her mandate sank in.

"I aim to provide that comprehensive accountability through an investigation of ceaseless rigour in dismantling enabling factors, toxic incentives and potential statutory reforms. Consider this a full diagnostic on FDA's house to determine how extensively the termites compromised our structural integrity."

Reporters immediately began peppering Bioren with questions about the scope of her investigative authorities and resources. But the prosecutor remained evasive, making clear only that her dragnet would extend across all FDA offices and that she'd been granted unilateral subpoena power to compel evidence and testimony as required.

"I will follow every thread and avert any potential cover-up without fear or institutional favour," Bioren stated bluntly. "Sunlight is and always will be the great disinfectant against systemic bureaucratic failings. Rest assured the examination ahead will be both searching and merciless to that end."

Bioren's no-nonsense team set about thoroughly reviewing every interaction between Zooth and FDA officials, from clinical trial oversight to reports documenting Neuroloxyn's deadly post-market impacts. An army of forensic auditors and data analysts meticulously charted the evidence trail, untangling every suspicious trigger along the way that may have been suppressed, waived or simply overlooked through negligence.

Much like the labyrinthine Zooth prosecutions before it, the investigative web kept expanding outward from every new incriminating revelation uncovered — improper communications, falsified safety data submissions, missing adverse event reports, whistleblowers bullied into silence or termination.

By the investigation's nadir, Bioren and her team had identified over 50 staffers across multiple levels and operational units who were ultimately referred for termination proceedings. Some were caught red-handed taking bribes from Zooth to bury negative findings; others were simply grossly negligent in conducting required oversight roles.

However, what may be most damning for the agency's credibility are indications that several senior-level FDA administrators not only turned a blind eye to mounting signals of Zooth's malfeasance but also actively participated in obstructing the oversight channels designed to provide accountability

In the final Bioren Report's scathing summation, words like "institutional rot" and "inbred criminal contempt" were highlighted for FDA's cultural descent into a "captive regulatory force" coopted to service the vested corporate interests it was intended to objectively police.

Ultimately, Bioren's recommendations included mass terminations, prosecutions and more broadly reforming FDA funding sources and statutory authorities to insulate the critical public mission from infiltration and overt regulatory capture moving forward.

Commissioner Rifkin swiftly enacted the proposed

remedies, and loudly championed new federal legislation providing FDA enhanced oversight teeth — including the ability to criminally charge executives obstructing drug safety monitoring or prematurely rushing new medicines to market.

Yet even as Bioren's reforms helped partially stanch the haemorrhaging credibility bleed, the human toll from the regulatory failures enabling Zooth's crimes lingered — an anguished legacy of emboldened public mistrust that would remain carved into FDA's soul for generations still to come.

For Bioren herself, there was simply resignation that her role in disrupting the systemic malignancy would remain ongoing in some capacity or another.

"The American public will forever demand proof in both word and deed that its core health protectors remain ethically insusceptible to the very grifters we're meant to police," she acknowledged wearily.

"So whether by my own hand or successor custodians yet unknown, this continual exorcism of unchecked greed's venom from our bureaucratic institutions must remain society's eternal vigil."

CHAPTER TWENTY

The Birth of a New Era

AS THE DUST began to settle and the smoke cleared, big Pharma found themselves standing at the precipice of a new era, one in which the once-untouchable titans of the pharmaceutical industry would be held accountable, and the sacred trust between healers and patients would be restored.

In the weeks and months that followed, their work bore fruit in ways they could scarcely have imagined. New legislation was enacted, designed to usher in an era of transparency and accountability within the pharmaceutical industry. Whistleblower protections were strengthened, and the cosy relationships between regulatory bodies and corporate interests were subjected to intense scrutiny.

But perhaps most importantly, a cultural shift began to take root. The public once resigned to the notion that profits would always take precedence over patient safety, found their voices and demanded change.

Jessica, David, and Amelia became icons of this movement, their names synonymous with a crusade that had not only exposed corruption but had also ignited a fire of righteous indignation that could not be extinguished.

They were no longer just doctors and journalists; they were symbols of hope, beacons of light that had pierced the darkness and illuminated a path towards a future where the pursuit of healing and the sanctity of human life would be elevated above the insatiable hunger for profits.

As they stood together, basking in the glow of their hard-won victory, they knew that the road ahead would be long and arduous. The forces they had challenged were still vast and deeply entrenched, their tentacles reaching into the highest echelons of power and influence.

But in that moment, they also knew that they had achieved something far greater than a mere exposé or a legal victory. They had struck a blow against the very heart of the corruption that had festered within the medical establishment, and in doing so, had ignited a spark of hope that would burn brightly for generations to come.

For in the shadows of the mind, a battle had been waged — a battle that had tested their resolve, their courage, and their unwavering commitment to the principles that had guided them from the outset. And though the scars of that battle would forever mark their souls, they wore them as badges of honour, a testament to the sacrifices they had made in pursuit of a higher calling.

As they turned their gaze towards the horizon, they knew that their work was far from over. New challenges would arise, new battles would be fought, and the forces of greed and corruption would inevitably rally, seeking to regain the ground they had lost.

But in that moment, they were victors, warriors

who had emerged from the crucible of their crusade with a renewed sense of purpose and a steely determination to continue the fight, no matter the obstacles that lay ahead.

For in the end, they had proven that the truth was a force unto itself, a weapon more powerful than any that could be wielded by the agents of greed and deceit. And as they looked to the future, they knew that their legacy would be one of hope, a shining beacon that would guide generations to come in the never-ending struggle to uphold the sanctity of human life and the principles that had once drawn them to the noble pursuit of healing.

OTHER BOOKS BY AUTHOR

Elsa

Ocean of Chance

New Girl

SHARE YOUR EXPERIENCE

Dear Esteemed Reader,

I am thrilled to extend my deepest gratitude to you for selecting my book from the vast array of options available. Your decision to embark on this literary journey fills my heart with profound appreciation and excitement.

As you immerse yourself in the pages of this book, I hope you find yourself transported into the world I've crafted, drawn to the characters, and engaged by the unfolding narrative. Your experience as a reader is invaluable, and I would be honoured if you could spare a moment to share your thoughts.

Reviews serve as the lifeblood of any writer's career. They offer not only invaluable feedback but also guide other readers in discovering this book amidst the multitude of options available. Whether you choose to share a brief sentiment or provide a detailed analysis, your honest opinion holds immeasurable significance.

If the book resonates with you, I kindly invite you to consider leaving a review on the platform where you acquired or encountered this book. Your support in spreading the word would be immensely appreciated.

Conversely, if the book did not meet your expectations, I welcome your constructive criticism. Such feedback enables me to evolve and improve as a writer, ensuring that future works better align with the desires of my readers.

Once again, I extend my sincerest gratitude for your time, attention, and willingness to embark on this literary voyage with me. Your support fuels my passion for storytelling, and I am deeply grateful for each reader who joins me on this adventure.

Warm regards,

Phoenix Lovegrove

Author of Justice and Atonement